ROMANCING

The kingdoms of Montebello and Tamir
are at peace. Montebello's missing prince
and heir is finally safe at home.
With both kingdoms rejoicing,
what could possibly go wrong?

Princess Samira Kamal: Her unfortunate
affair with a Montebellan royal has ended
in despair—and pregnancy. Marriage to her
enigmatic bodyguard offers refuge—and
unexpected passion....

Farid Nasir: He is bound by duty and honor not
to touch his royal wife. But desire never plays
by the rules in affairs of the heart....

Desmond Caruso: Though royal by blood, his
illegitimacy keeps him outside the Montebellan
inner circle. Now his ruthless thirst for power
brings him everything he deserves.

Sheik Ahmed and Queen Alima Kamal: Their
daughter's condition and secret marriage shock
them, but the truth would shock them more.

Ursula Chambers: Is the mysterious blonde the
cause of all Samira and Farid's troubles? Or is
she another of Desmond's victims?

Dear Reader,

It's August, and our books are as hot as the weather, so if it's romantic excitement you crave, look no further. Merline Lovelace is back with the newest CODE NAME: DANGER title, *Texas Hero*. Reunion romances are always compelling, because emotions run high. Add the spice of danger and you've got the perfection of the relationship between Omega agent Jack Carstairs and heroine-in-danger Ellie Alazar.

ROMANCING THE CROWN continues with Carla Cassidy's *Secrets of a Pregnant Princess*, a marriage-of-convenience story featuring Tamiri princess Samira Kamal and her mysterious bodyguard bridegroom. Marie Ferrarella brings us another of THE BACHELORS OF BLAIR MEMORIAL in *M.D. Most Wanted*, giving the phrase "doctor-patient confidentiality" a whole new meaning. Award-winning New Zealander Frances Housden makes her second appearance in the line with *Love Under Fire*, and her fellow Kiwi Laurey Bright checks in with *Shadowing Shahna*. Finally, wrap up the month with Jenna Mills and her latest, *When Night Falls*.

Next month, return to Intimate Moments for more fabulous reading—including the newest from bestselling author Sharon Sala, *The Way to Yesterday*. Until then…enjoy!

Yours,

Leslie J. Wainger
Executive Senior Editor

Please address questions and book requests to:
Silhouette Reader Service
U.S.: 3010 Walden Ave., P.O. Box 1325, Buffalo, NY 14269
Canadian: P.O. Box 609, Fort Erie, Ont. L2A 5X3

Secrets of a
Pregnant Princess
CARLA CASSIDY

INTIMATE MOMENTS™

Published by Silhouette Books

America's Publisher of Contemporary Romance

Special thanks and acknowledgment are given to Carla Cassidy for her contribution to the ROMANCING THE CROWN series.

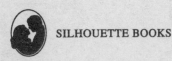

SILHOUETTE BOOKS

ISBN 0-373-27236-7

SECRETS OF A PREGNANT PRINCESS

Visit Silhouette at www.eHarlequin.com

Printed in U.S.A.

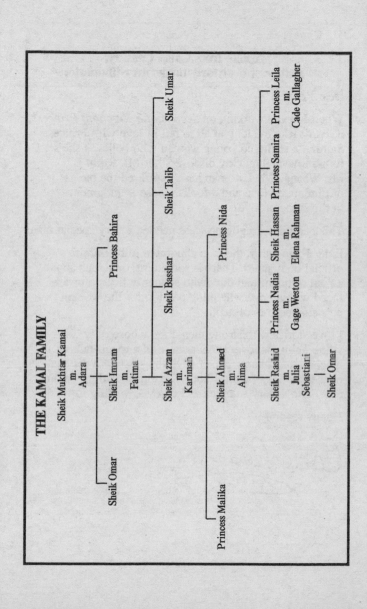

THE KAMAL FAMILY

Sheik Mukhtar Kamal
m.
Adara

- Sheik Omar
- Sheik Imram
  m.
  Fatima
  - Princess Bahira
  - Sheik Azzam
    m.
    Karimah
    - Sheik Basshar
    - Sheik Talib
    - Sheik Umar
- Sheik Ahmed
  m.
  Alima
  - Princess Malika
  - Princess Nida
  - Sheik Rashid
    m.
    Julia
    Sebastiari
    - Sheik Omar
  - Princess Nadia
    m.
    Gage Weston
  - Sheik Hassan
    m.
    Elena Rahman
  - Princess Samira
  - Princess Leila
    m.
    Cade Gallagher

A note from Carla Cassidy,
author of over forty books for Silhouette:

Dear Reader,

When I began working on *Secrets of a Pregnant Princess*, it didn't take me long at all to fall in love with Princess Samira, a sheltered young woman who believes she's found love and quickly discovers her Mr. Right is Mr. Wrong. What woman hasn't suffered the pangs of unrequited love and a foolish lapse in judgment in the name of love?

This beautiful, fragile princess needed a very special man.

Enter Farid Nasir, the man appointed to be Samira's official bodyguard. There is something delicious about a man of honor and duty who suddenly finds himself faced with an overwhelming passion for the woman he's supposed to protect.

I love stories with strong men, men whose only vulnerability is love. Having married a tough-talking, macho man, I know personally how sweet are the centers of these kinds of men. I hope you enjoy reading Samira and Farid's story as much as I enjoyed writing it.

Happy reading!

Carla Cassidy

Chapter 1

Princess Samira Kamal clutched the ends of her armrests as the small, private jet began its descent. Take-offs or landings—she wasn't sure which she hated more.

"May I get you something, Princess?"

Samira looked at the man seated directly across from her. Farid Nasir...her bodyguard. Even here, on her father's private jet with no one else in the plane but the crew, Farid was on alert with no relaxation in any part of his firmly muscled body.

"No, thank you. I'm fine," she replied and turned her attention to the window where the island of Montebello had come into view.

It wasn't a long flight from her country of Tamir to the neighboring island of Montebello, but this flight had seemed endless. Each moment had been sheer agony since she'd made the decision to fly to Montebello and meet Desmond Caruso.

She shot a glance at her traveling companion. Farid had been her bodyguard for less than three months, but in that time she hadn't seen him crack a smile or display any hint of a sense of humor.

She would concede that he was handsome, with his short raven hair and firmly chiseled features. He had beautiful eyes, dark brown with thick, long lashes. However, they were cold…soulless, never giving a hint of the man within.

She dismissed thoughts of Farid as the wheels of the small royal jet hit the runway. If things went as she planned during this visit to Montebello, she wouldn't need her father to provide her with a bodyguard. She would have a husband to provide all that she needed.

A slight trepidation shot through her as she realized that within the next hour she would see Desmond again. Surely all her dreams were about to come true. She and Desmond would marry and hopefully live happily ever after.

She closed her eyes, remembering how it had felt to be in Desmond's arms, imagining how wonderful it would be to be his wife for the rest of her life.

She'd spoken to him on the phone only the week before and he'd told her how much he missed her, how much he wished they could be together. He'd told her he thought of her day and night and longed for the time they could be together again. He had to be the right man for her. He just had to be!

"Princess…"

She frowned at the interruption into her pleasant daydreams. Opening her eyes, she saw Farid standing up, waiting patiently for her attention.

"There is a car waiting to take you to the palace."

"Yes, of course." She stood and allowed Farid to escort her off the plane and into the limo with a miniature Montebellan black, white and gold flag flying from its antenna.

Farid didn't sit back in the seat and relax, but rather sat forward, his gaze going from window to window with the alertness of a big cat on the prowl.

As usual, he was stoically silent on the brief ride from the airstrip to the massive grounds of the royal palace. Just once she'd like to see what his face looked like with a smile curving his lips, with warmth shining from his eyes.

Since he'd been assigned as her personal bodyguard, she'd found him not only to have more than his share of arrogance, but also to be exceptionally good at his job. It was the latter quality that had her worried.

Somehow, someway, in the next couple of hours she desperately needed to escape Farid's watchful eyes to rendezvous with Desmond. She did not want to meet her lover with her bodyguard hovering nearby. She needed time alone with Desmond, time to tell him her news, time for them to make the plans that would seal their future together.

Within minutes they had passed through the guarded gates of the palace grounds. The car pulled up in front of the impressive entrance to the grand palace.

Set on top of a cliff overlooking the sea, the palace was a two-story whitewashed stucco and marble with traditional Mediterranean touches. A large fountain was set amid lush greenery in front of the palace, giving it an added touch of elegance and grandeur.

As they stepped out of the car, Samira could instantly smell the salt brine in the air, could hear the distant sound of waves breaking against the jagged rocks at the base of the cliff where the palace was located.

They entered a large, marble-floored entry with cathedral-height ceilings and ornate gold trim. A butler, who introduced himself as Rudolpho Sabira, led them up the grand staircase to the private quarters of King Marcus Sebastiani and his wife, Queen Gwendolyn.

Samira couldn't help but think that if all went well with Desmond, she would be related to the king and queen of Montebello through marriage, as was her brother Rashid.

"Princess Samira." The lovely Queen Gwendolyn took her hands and greeted her warmly. "It's such a pleasure to have you here as our guest."

"Thank you," Samira replied, then looked at the white-haired king who stood next to the queen. "King Marcus, my father sends his regards."

"And they are returned," King Marcus said. "I understand you've come to explore the beauty of our island."

"Yes. I was quite captured by the beauty of Montebello the last time I was here and thought it would be a perfect spot to spend a week of vacation time. I'm also eager to visit with Princess Anna. I so enjoyed spending time with her when you were all in Tamir for my brother Hassan's wedding.''

''Ah, yes.'' King Marcus's eyes lit with obvious affection as he thought of his youngest daughter. ''Unfortunately, Anna is not in residence at the moment. She and her new husband, Tyler Ramsey, are spending some time in the United States.''

Samira had known before she left Tamir that Anna wasn't in Montebello, a fact her own father had been unaware of. When she'd told her father, Sheik Ahmed Kamal, that she wanted to go to Montebello to visit Anna and to explore the sights of the island, he'd given his blessing, knowing how much she enjoyed Princess Anna's vivaciousness and enthusiasm for life.

''I'm so sorry to learn she isn't here,'' Samira exclaimed, hoping she sounded genuinely surprised at the news.

''However, the beauty of Montebello awaits you and we have put you in one of the private guest quarters on the ground. We hope you'll be most comfortable,'' King Marcus continued.

''I'm sure you'd like to freshen up after your trip.'' A tiny wrinkle appeared in Queen Gwendolyn's forehead. ''Has your maid traveled with you or would you like us to provide you one for the duration of your visit?''

''No, thank you but that won't be necessary,''

Samira demurred. "Actually, I'm looking forward to the novelty of taking care of myself for the duration of this trip."

"Then we won't keep you," Queen Gwendolyn said. "The cottage is fully serviced with staff who take care of the cleaning and delivery of meals. Anything you need, don't hesitate to ask. Perhaps you will join us for dinner later in the week."

"I would be most honored," Samira replied.

"The driver is waiting to take you to your quarters," King Marcus finished.

A few moments later Farid and Samira were back in the car, being driven to the private cottage where they would stay for the rest of the visit.

"Oh, how nice," Samira exclaimed as they got out of the car in front of the guest house. The cottage itself was a white stucco, surrounded by lush, heavily perfumed flowers and deep-green bushes. It looked like an enchanted cottage from a fairy tale.

They walked into a luxurious living room decorated in blues and golds. The furniture was oversized, a sofa with mounds of throw pillows and two matching chairs set on a gorgeous Oriental rug. A basket of luscious fruit sat on the coffee table and fresh flower arrangements scented the air with their sweet fragrance.

A king-size bed graced the master bedroom, along with a sitting area, a stately dresser and a lavish bathroom.

The second bedroom was considerably smaller with a half bath. There was also a kitchenette with every convenience known to mankind for those who preferred privacy instead of taking their meals in the dining room in the palace or having them delivered in.

"I think I'll just freshen up and unpack," Samira said to Farid. He acknowledged her words with a curt nod of his head and she disappeared into the master bedroom and closed the door behind her.

Her suitcases were on the floor where the driver had placed them, but she opened only one, her cosmetic case. She would freshen up, then slip away from Farid and find Desmond, she hoped.

She stared at her reflection in the mirror, wondering if she needed to touch up her blush. Her cheeks were pink with excitement and her dark eyes sparkled with the exhilaration that bubbled inside her.

Desmond. Desmond, her heart cried out. She hoped she was only mere minutes away from her destiny, her heart's desire. Surely Desmond was her heart's desire? She frowned and shoved aside the niggling doubt.

For the past few months it seemed that love had blossomed for everyone around her. She'd watched all her brothers and sisters find love, and had yearned to find it for herself. There was nothing she wanted more than to be a wife and nurture her own family.

Hopefully, before this night was over, that was what her immediate future would hold. With a hand that trembled slightly, she brushed her shoulder-length dark hair, put on a fresh layer of lipstick, then spritzed herself with her favorite perfume.

She stepped back and looked at herself critically.

Maybe she should change clothes. The coral-colored long dress complemented her olive complexion, but it was slightly wrinkled from traveling. Smoothing her hand over the wrinkles, she decided she didn't want to take the time to change.

She was ready...all she needed was an escape route. She knew without a doubt that Farid would not be in his room with the door closed. He was far too conscientious for that. He would be sitting or standing in the living room, like a shadow, watching her movements and anticipating danger at every corner.

She frowned thoughtfully and walked over to the window in front of the sitting area in the bedroom. Her heart gave a joyous leap as she realized the window had a latch, which meant it opened and closed.

As she turned the latch and pulled it open, she recognized that what she was about to do was completely out of character for her. She was not adventurous or bold. In truth, most of the time she feared herself rather boring. But love gave her courage, hope made her bold, and once the window was open, she removed the screen and climbed out.

A new exhilaration filled her as she stepped outside and drew in a breath of the sweet-scented night air. Darkness was falling and the moon overhead was a silver ball shining down a lover's light.

Escape had been ridiculously easy, and she felt as if fate was making it simple for her to claim the future she so desired.

The next step was to find Desmond. She knew he had quarters on the palace grounds, but she also knew the palace grounds were immense. Unsure in which direction to go, she took off walking, following a cobblestone sidewalk that she hoped would take her to a guard.

Sure enough, after only a few minutes, she ran into a palace guard who gave her directions to Desmond's private quarters.

She had met Desmond Caruso, King Marcus's handsome nephew, almost three months before at her brother Hassan's wedding to Elena Rahmon. Desmond had swept her off her feet with his incredible looks and seductive charm.

He'd spent a week in Tamir, and during that week he and Samira had met whenever possible, snatching glorious moments in secret trysts.

Desmond had looked at her as no other man had in her life. He'd listened to her hopes and dreams, encouraged her to open up to him and had opened up to her about his unhappy childhood. She'd felt an immediate connection, and he'd told her he felt it, too.

She had surrendered her innocence to him. They had made love twice, and while she'd found the act of lovemaking not particularly pleasant, she'd told herself it was because she was inexperienced, and that that part of their relationship would improve with time.

"And we'll have a lifetime of lovemaking," she murmured aloud, her heart singing with joy.

If Farid had been her bodyguard three months ago when she'd met Desmond, she probably would have never gotten any opportunity to be alone with Desmond.

But her brother's wedding had taken place in Tamir, and Samira's entire family had attended. There had been royal guards all around, but no personal bodyguards for Samira and her sisters.

Would Desmond be happy to see her? This trip had been an impromptu one and she hadn't told him she'd be arriving tonight. But he must have heard she was coming.

Of course he'll be happy to see you, she told herself firmly. He loves you, he told you so only last week. He'd promised that as soon as he got an opportunity to speak to her father, they would be married.

Her heart quickened once again as she came to the guest house where the guard had told her Desmond lived. Across from the guest house a fountain gurgled, as if proclaiming Samira's future in bubbling glee.

The small house sat just off the sidewalk. Like her guest quarters, it was surrounded by bushes laden with lush pink flowers that scented the balmy night air.

She hesitated a moment on the sidewalk and drew a deep breath to steady herself. At that moment, she heard the soft murmur of voices drifting out from a partially open front window.

He wasn't alone. She didn't want to burst in on him and deliver her exciting news if he wasn't alone. She moved to a position just behind a large, neatly trimmed bush where she could easily peek into the window.

She just wanted to get a glimpse of the man she planned to spend her future with. Just a quick peek at his beloved, handsome face.

She froze as her mind grappled to make sense of the scene before her. Desmond stood directly in her line of vision. He was clad in a pair of dark slacks and a tailored white shirt, and his dark hair glistened in the overhead light.

He definitely was not alone. Locked in his arms was a long-legged, tawny blonde wearing a short red dress that exposed long, shapely legs.

A sister...a cousin...Samira's mind worked for a logical explanation. But, as she saw Desmond's hands move sensually down the woman's back to grab her buttocks, as he lowered his head and took her mouth with his, Samira knew the woman was no sister or cousin. She was obviously Desmond's lover.

His lover.

A sharp pain exploded in her heart, and somewhere in the back of her mind she recognized it as the shattering of hopes and dreams.

He'd told her she was the only woman in his life. Only last week he'd told her how much he loved her, how lonely he was without her. He'd told her he counted the hours until they would be together again. He'd said so many things, so many sweet, wonderful things.

Lies. All lies.

Samira stumbled backward a step and tried desperately to contain the wrenching sob that begged to be released.

She didn't want to see any more, yet couldn't tear her gaze away from the sight of the man whom she'd believed loved her kissing and caressing another woman.

Someplace in the back of her mind, she knew she needed to escape, before Desmond saw her, before she completely humiliated herself. But her feet refused to listen to her brain, and she remained frozen in place as her heart broke into a million pieces.

From the moment they boarded the private jet, Farid Nasir knew that something was up with Samira. Throughout his years of working for the Kamal family, he'd watched Samira grow from a shy, unimposing young girl into a gentle, caring woman known for her warmth and openness.

But on the plane ride, he'd seen a tension in her that had nothing to do with her dislike for flying. Her dark, long-lashed, almond-shaped eyes had snapped with secrets…and secrets worried Farid.

She'd told her father, Sheik Ahmed, that she was coming to Montebello to visit with Princess Anna, but her exclamation of surprise at learning that Princess Anna was absent from Montebello hadn't rung true.

He now sat in a chair in the corner of the living room, waiting for Samira to finish freshening up and unpacking. It was just after nine, and he'd had to turn on a lamp against the encroaching darkness of night.

Looking at his watch, he frowned. She'd now been in the bedroom for more than twenty minutes, and he'd heard no sound from the room in the past fifteen.

He knew she hadn't gone to bed. The one thing he'd learned in the past two and a half months of being personally assigned as her bodyguard was that Princess Samira liked to stay up late and loved to sleep in during the morning hours.

Again a disquieting unease crept through him. Instinct told him something was wrong, and Farid never ignored his instincts.

He got up from his chair and went to her bedroom door. He hesitated a moment, then knocked. "Princess Samira?"

There was no reply. No sound whatsoever seeped through the wooden door. No light shone from beneath the door, either.

She couldn't be unpacking and freshening up in the darkness, he thought. The unease kicked up a notch, transforming into real concern.

He knocked again and when there was still no answer, he twisted the knob and eased open the door.

The room held a stillness that indicated emptiness. "Princess Samira?" he said softly, then turned on the overhead light.

Immediately he spied the open window with the screen removed. Horror riveted through him. He raced to the window. Had somebody ripped the screen away to kidnap Samira? Was she now being held someplace for ransom? For political purposes? Farid knew as well as anyone that there were terrorist groups that always posed a threat to the members of the royal family.

Fear, icy-cold and sickening, filled him. A fear that

turned to rage as he realized the screen could not be removed from the outside, but only from the inside.

That meant Samira herself had removed the screen and disappeared into the encroaching shadows of the night.

Why? The question rang in his head as he raced out of the house. He hesitated on the sidewalk, unsure of which direction to go. He had to find her. As a princess of Tamir, she should not be wandering around alone.

Dammit, she knew better than to go off on her own, he thought as he hurried down the sidewalk. His gaze swept left, then right as he ran, searching for any sign of the princess under his protection.

Sheik Ahmed would have his head if anything happened to his beloved daughter. And Farid would not be able to live with himself.

He knew the palace grounds were huge, and he had no idea if he was going in the right direction. As he hurried along, he encountered two palace guards. The first one had seen nobody all evening long. The second guard told him he'd given Princess Samira directions to Desmond Caruso's quarters and gave the same directions to Farid.

Farid ran, knowing that as long as Samira was alone she was in possible danger. As he raced in the direction the guard had indicated, his anger peaked into a new burst of rage.

What had possessed her? Had this entire trip to Montebello been about a romantic liaison? If so, it was the most irresponsible thing she'd ever done.

He breathed a sigh of relief as he spied her familiar, petite shape standing on the sidewalk just outside Desmond Caruso's residence.

Although her back was to him, he recognized the bright coral dress that hugged her slender shape. He grabbed her by the shoulders and whirled her around to face him.

"How dare you compromise my position and your own safety by sneaking out?" he exclaimed angrily.

Her beautiful eyes widened at the sight of him, then she burst into tears. He instantly dropped his hands from her shoulders.

"And don't think your tears will temper my anger with you at the moment," he continued irritably. "I will not be manipulated by your tears. What you did was foolish and irresponsible."

"You have no idea just how foolish and irresponsible I've been," she cried, and before Farid knew her intent, she threw herself against him, sobbing as if her heart was breaking in two.

Desmond Caruso was irritated, but he hid his irritation beneath the charming smile that was his trademark. It wasn't enough that in the last couple of weeks he'd felt himself being subtly cut off from all palace gossip and news, now he had Ursula to deal with.

"Ursula...darling...give me a minute to breathe." Gently, but firmly, he moved away from the slender, busty blonde.

Ursula Chambers had been the last person he'd expected to show up at his place, although he'd known she was in Montebello.

Over the past week he'd received numerous messages and phone calls from her, but he'd accepted none of them. He had bigger fish to fry than a failed actress with desperation in her eyes.

He had met Ursula almost five months before when he'd traveled to Shady Rock, Colorado to get information about King Marcus's eldest son and heir to the throne, Prince Lucas. It had been more than a year since Lucas's plane had gone down in the Rockies.

Although the wreckage had been thoroughly searched, as had the area in and around the crash site, no body had ever been found.

Desmond had received information that it was possible the crown prince had worked as a ranch hand on a small spread in Shady Rock, so he had flown to Colorado to check it out. There he'd met Ursula, and instantly he'd recognized her as a kindred spirit.

"You've been avoiding me," she now said, her plump lips pulled into a pout.

"That's not true," he protested. "I've just been so busy." He'd been busy romancing a princess from Tamir. A man had to do what a man had to do in order to achieve his plans for his future. "But you were never far from my mind. By the way, how did you get past the guards?"

Ursula sank down on the sofa and crossed her long, shapely legs. "It took me almost every night of the last week to finally convince a guard to let me in." She smiled and twirled a strand of her long hair between two fingers. "It took a combination of seductive flirting, money and the promise of more of both to come before he'd tell me where you lived and let me in."

"And who was this guard who takes his job so seriously?" Desmond asked. He would see to it that the guard was fired for dereliction of duty.

"Edwardo something…"

"Edwardo Scarpa." Desmond knew the guard well. Scarpa had a weakness for women and many suspected a bit of a gambling habit.

Ursula dropped the strand of her hair and leaned forward, her blue eyes as guileless as a newborn baby. "But let's not talk about him. Let's talk about us."

There is no us, Desmond wanted to yell. There had been a time when he'd actively pursued Ursula, a time when he'd believed her useful to his goals.

Believing she had information about the missing crown prince, he'd become her lover and confidante.

However, since Prince Lucas had returned alive and well and Desmond's hopes of seeing his half brother, Lorenzo, on the throne had been dashed, he no longer had any use for the striking, scheming has-been actress.

But he also realized it would be dangerous to toss her out like a piece of spoiled meat. She knew too much, and it was possible that if he spurned her she would make trouble for him.

He sat on the sofa next to her and placed his arm around her. Her scent surrounded him, the scent of expensive perfume. She held herself stiffly for a mo-

ment, the innocence in her eyes transforming into
something almost ugly. "I shouldn't even speak to
you, much less let you touch me. You've been mean
and hateful in ignoring me. I will not be ignored,
Desmond."

Her words, subtle with an unspoken threat, fired
his irritation once again, but he smiled and stroked a
hand down the softness of her hair. "Darling, I told
you I haven't been ignoring you. Since Prince Lucas's
return, there has been much business to attend to here
in Montebello."

The anger left her eyes, replaced by an edge of
desperation. "So, you still want me?"

"Of course I do." He pulled her closer and kissed
her eager lips.

As the kiss ended she sighed with pleasure and
smiled at him, a new twinkle in her eyes. "I had to
come to see you. I missed you so much…and I have
some information for you."

"Information?" Desmond sat back. "What kind of
information?"

Her lips curved into a smug, secretive smile. "Information that just might be worth a king's ransom."

Desmond's pulse quickened. "What are you talking about? Tell me."

Again her lips puffed out in a pout. "I don't think
I'll tell you now, you've been so mean in not returning my phone calls and messages."

Desmond clenched his fists in frustration. Damn
this woman and her foolish games. He knew she

wouldn't have traveled all this way if she didn't think the information she had was valuable.

Ursula was looking for the same things Desmond was...a future filled with riches, and a place among royalty. And like himself, he knew she would stop at nothing to get what she wanted.

"How many times do I have to tell you, I've been busy. I was not intentionally avoiding you. Now, tell me what this tidbit of information is."

She shook her head, a glassy glitter hardening her gaze. "I think you should take me out for dinner tomorrow evening. Someplace nice and expensive...someplace where I'll be seen by important people. Then perhaps I'll share my secret with you."

She stood, looking like the proverbial cat that had dined on the canary. "I'm staying at the Montebello hotel, room 212. I'll expect you about seven tomorrow evening."

Desmond stood, fighting against his desire to wrap his hands around her slender neck and throttle her until her face turned blue. However, before he could do that, he had to learn the secret she possessed that was worth a "king's ransom."

Once he got that secret out of her, he would see to it that he was rid of her forever, and her permanent silence was assured.

Chapter 2

Other than an occasional inadvertent brush of shoulders or the accidental touching of hands, Farid had never before touched Princess Samira. Now they stood breasts to chest, hip to hip.

He had never considered before how soft her breasts might be against his own chest. He had never before considered how neatly the top of her head would fit so perfectly beneath his chin.

The spicy scent of her perfume was intoxicating, as were the soft curves that filled his arms. Farid drew in a sharp breath as he realized the thoughts that flittered at the edges of his mind were distinctly unbodyguardlike.

For just a moment, he wanted to wrap her in his arms. He wanted to tangle his fingers into her shoulder-length, silky black hair and taste the sweetness of her full lips.

These thoughts were fleeting and completely inappropriate. Instead of following through on any of them, he once again gripped her by her slender shoulders and pulled her away from him.

Her tears had now changed to deep, wrenching sobs. "I don't know what I'm going to do...I've been so incredibly stupid...how am I ever going to tell my parents..." The words came jerkily from her, interspersed with choking sobs.

He'd thought her tears to be an attempt at manipulation so he wouldn't stay angry with her. Now he recognized them as something much different, and a touch of alarm shot through him.

What could be so bad that she couldn't go to her parents?

A million questions filled his head, but as he saw several royal guards wearing expressions of concern walking in their direction, he took her arm. "Princess, pull yourself together," he commanded brusquely. It would not do to create a scandal.

The answers to his questions could be told to him when they were back in their private quarters. This was not the time or the place.

Still holding her arm, he guided her away from Desmond Caruso's residence and back toward the guest house where they were staying. He nodded curtly to the guards, apparently satisfying them that everything was under control.

Neither of them spoke on the way back to their

quarters. The only sounds were those of the singing of night insects and Samira's soft crying.

Once they were again in the guest house, she sank down on the overstuffed cushions of the sofa and buried her face in her hands.

Again concern filled Farid. He stood directly before her. "Princess...do you wish to talk about whatever it is that has you distressed?" Aware of his position as her servant, not her equal, he was reluctant to push her too hard.

She looked up at him, her dark eyes liquid with tears and the tip of her nose slightly reddened by her crying. "What is there to talk about?" Her voice held a slight edge of hysteria. "I loved him. I thought he loved me...hc told me he loved me, but he lied. It was all lies."

Farid relaxed as he realized the reason for her tears was apparently nothing more than a foolish matter of the heart. Women, he thought. Such passionate, emotional creatures.

Farid had never been bothered with such nonsense. He'd had women before...physical relationships that were pleasant, but with women who expected nothing from him, women who knew his life, his honor and his heart were bound to Sheik Ahmed Kamal and the Tamiri crown.

"Who told you he loved you?" he asked curiously. "Desmond Caruso?"

She nodded, her silky dark hair partially obscuring her delicate features as she stared down at her folded hands in her lap. "I thought we were going to get married. He led me to believe we'd have a life together. I thought he was the man for me." Once again tears fell from her eyes and trekked down her cheeks. "He told me I was the only woman for him, but he lied. He was with somebody else just now...his lover."

Farid frowned, unsure how to handle this uncustomary display of emotion. In the months he had been with Samira, she'd always been cheerful and optimistic, never given to dramatic outbursts.

"Then the man is a snake and you'll find another man who will marry you," he said gruffly. He wanted nothing more than for her to stop crying.

"No, I won't," she cried miserably. She jumped up off the sofa and walked to the window, looking like a wilted, peach-colored flower. "You don't understand," she said, her back to him. "No man will ever want me now."

He stared at her in bewilderment. "Don't be silly. You're an attractive young woman and I'm certain you will have many suitors in your future."

"I'm not a young woman," she protested, her back still to him. "I'm twenty-nine years old and no other man will ever want me because...because..." She twirled around and looked at him, sheer misery reflected in the darkness of her eyes. "I'm pregnant with Desmond's child."

Farid sucked in a gasp of shock. Pregnant? How was that possible? He couldn't remember a time when she'd been out of his sight. When had she had the opportunity to meet privately with Desmond Caruso... privately enough to make love?

Had Farid been less than vigilant in his duties? Had there been a time when Princess Samira had been out of his sight? "How...when?"

"Don't look so worried," she said dryly, finally managing to get her tears under control. She swiped quickly at her eyes with the back of one hand, then looked at him. "It happened before my father assigned you to me. It was when Desmond came to Tamir for Hassan's wedding."

Although her words did nothing to alleviate the problem, a small wave of relief swept through Farid. At least he knew he hadn't fallen down in his duties. "Then we must return to Tamir immediately and speak to your father," he said. "He and your mother should know about this."

"No!" she said emphatically. She left the window and walked quickly to stand before him. She reached out and grabbed his hand. "Please, Farid, we can't tell my father. You know how old-fashioned he and my mother are. He'll force Desmond to marry me...or he'll arrange a marriage to the son of one of his friends and I'll just die if that happens."

She looked so small, so achingly vulnerable with her full lower lip quivering and her beautiful eyes luminous with new tears. A wave of protectiveness surged through him, and he wanted nothing more than to physically pound Desmond Caruso to the ground.

The man had obviously taken advantage of

Samira's naïveté, manipulated her emotions and abused her innocence.

Farid knew she was right. Sheik Ahmed would not tolerate this kind of dishonor and would demand an instant remedy. And the remedy would, in all probability, be marriage to Desmond Caruso. If Caruso refused, new tensions would arise between the countries of Tamir and Montebello. At the moment the two countries were enjoying relatively good relations, but something like this could destroy the tenuous peace.

She released his hand and once again sank to the sofa. With one hand she traced the gold threads that accented the blue sofa material. "I will not marry that man. I hope...I pray I never, ever have to see him again."

He sat next to her, keeping a respectful distance and trying to ignore her spicy perfumed scent. He frowned, trying to find a solution to the mess Samira found herself in. "Perhaps there is a young man you are fond of, somebody you wouldn't mind being married to."

She shook her head. "There is nobody. You know I don't date often."

It was true, in the months since he'd been her bodyguard she hadn't had one date, although she had an active social life with friends.

He watched her trembling fingers tracing the golden threads of the armrest. She had long, delicate fingers, with nails painted a pale pearly pink. For some inexplicable reason, the sight of those

feminine fingernails sent a new burst of protectiveness through him.

His princess was in trouble, and it was his duty to
keep her safe. If she returned to Tamir pregnant and
unmarried, there would be a scandal. The tabloids
would have a field day with the news.

He stared at the wall opposite the sofa and thought
of the vow he'd made both to himself and to Sheik
Ahmed when he'd first come to work for the Kamal
family twelve years earlier as a twenty-year-old man.

He had pledged his heart, his soul and his very life
to protecting the Kamal family and that meant protecting them from scandal as well as from any physical harm.

And if that pledge hadn't been enough to make him
do what he was about to do, then a promise he'd made
seven months ago was enough…a promise made to a
man now dead, a man he'd known for far too brief a
time.

He looked back at Samira. It was his duty—perhaps his destiny—to take care of this situation. "If
you refuse to tell your parents the truth, then there is
only one other alternative that will make everything
all right."

Her gaze was suddenly hopeful as she looked at
him. "What?"

He didn't love her, didn't even believe in love. He
didn't really know her well at all, but knew none of
that mattered. He did know she was a good woman,
a woman whom others came to for advice, a woman
respected for having a soft heart and a listener's ear.

But none of that really mattered, either. He had to think about what was best not only for her, but for the child she carried.

"The answer is really quite simple," he said. "Marry me."

Samira stared at her handsome bodyguard, stunned by what he'd just offered. Impossible, she thought instantly, but, in the back of her mind she knew that marrying Farid would certainly alleviate some of the scandal that was certain to blossom when news of her pregnancy got out.

If she had the baby out of wedlock, not only would it be fodder for the gossipmongers and tabloids, it would also be a poor reflection on her parents.

Tears once again burned her eyes as she thought of her parents. They would be appalled by her lack of judgment, and she feared her father's legendary temper.

Marry Farid?

I wanted to marry for love, her heart cried out. All her life she'd embraced a fantasy of love that she'd believed one day would come true.

She knew nothing about Farid Nasir except that her father trusted him with her life.

Tears once again filled her eyes, and she swiped at them with two fingers. She'd always dreamed of a marriage proposal, but in her dreams it had been quite different.

Casting a surreptitious gaze at Farid, she wondered if it was possible that he cared about her just a little.

Was it possible that during the past two and a half months, he'd secretly fallen a little bit in love with her?

Don't be stupid, she chided herself inwardly. It was impossible to read him by merely looking at him. His facial features were as stoic as ever.

"I...I don't know what to say," she finally managed.

"It's a good plan," Farid said. "I realize I am but a mere servant and not worthy of a princess's hand in marriage—"

Although he said the words, there was a touch of arrogance to his tone that made Samira think that he truly believed he was more than worthy of a princess's hand.

He continued "—but I'll do whatever it takes to save you from disgrace, to protect the good name of your father and the crown. It is my job...my duty."

A new wave of despair swept through her. Of course, she should have known his offer of marriage had nothing to do with his heart and everything to do with duty.

She was fairly certain Farid Nasir had no heart. And as far as she was concerned, marrying him simply wasn't a viable option.

"Thank you, Farid." She looked down at her hands in her lap. "I'm sure my father would be pleased by your obvious devotion to him and the crown, but I cannot accept your proposal."

His dark brows rose up in obvious surprise. "What I am suggesting is a marriage in name only," he said.

"Of course there would be no...no intimacy between us. The marriage would be for the benefit of the child you carry, and for the sake of your honor."

She wondered if Farid had ever made love with a woman. Didn't lovemaking require some sort of feelings, some sort of emotions? She couldn't imagine Farid experiencing any sort of heightened emotions or passion that might lead to a bout of lovemaking.

"A marriage between us just isn't the solution," she said.

"Then what is the solution?"

She looked up and met his dark, brooding eyes. If she'd seen any hint of softness there, any sign of even the smallest affection or emotion of any kind, she might have relented.

But there was nothing there, and she once again looked down at her hands as she rolled his question around in her head. "I don't know," she replied softly. "I think what I need is to go to bed and sleep on it."

She was suddenly exhausted. What had begun as a trip of joy and expectation had suddenly become a study in heartache, the like of which she'd never suffered before.

She stood, and Farid did the same. "Before you go into the bedroom, I need to replace the screen in the window frame." She nodded and sat back down on the sofa as he disappeared into the bedroom.

He returned a few minutes later and stood rigidly at one side of the sofa. "Can I be assured that you won't slip out the window again?" he asked, his voice laced with the heavy displeasure her previous escape had apparently provoked in him.

"Trust me, you don't have to worry about me sneaking away from you ever again. Good night, Farid." She had almost reached the bedroom door when he called to her. She turned back to face him.

"The marriage proposal still stands," he said. "You will need somebody to take care of you and the child."

She wanted to protest, to say that she would be fine all by herself, but instead she just nodded, then escaped into the bedroom before tears could once again fall from her overburdened heart.

It took her only a few minutes to unpack and change into her long, silky nightgown. Then she stood in the bathroom and stared at her reflection in the mirror.

Pregnant. She was pregnant, and the man who was the father of the baby, the man she'd thought loved her above all others, was nothing but a snake in the grass.

He'd held her in his arms and lied to her. He'd stroked her naked body and lied to her. Every kiss, every caress and every promise had been a lie.

The promises he had made…she sighed miserably as she thought of the future Desmond had painted with his lies. He'd spoken of a house and a family, of children's laughter and passion-filled nights.

It had been the kind of future she'd dreamed of since she'd been a young child, the kind of future she'd longed for as a young woman. Lies. All lies.

She placed her hand on her tummy, where there wasn't as yet any telltale pouch, no indication whatsoever of the little soul growing within.

The obvious solution was a quiet, discreet abortion, but as far as Samira was concerned, that wasn't an option at all. She'd been raised to revere life, and no matter what she now thought of Desmond Caruso, she already loved the baby inside her with a fierceness that surprised even herself.

She left the bathroom, turned out all the lights and climbed beneath the soft, luxurious sheets of the king-size bed. Lying on her side facing the window, she could see the moon in the sky.

Where before the fat silvery orb had appeared to her to be a lover's moon, now it mocked her with its beauty. How could she tell her parents what she had done? How foolish she had been?

She could never tell them the name of the man who had impregnated her. She knew without a doubt her father would either see her married to Desmond, or have his head on a platter.

She wanted neither. She just wanted to forget Desmond Caruso. She sighed and forced her eyes to close. Nor did she want to marry Farid. She couldn't imagine being married even in name only to such a cold, emotionless man.

She didn't know what she wanted. In the best of worlds she would have arrived here in Montebello and delivered the news of her pregnancy to Desmond, who would have taken her in his arms and eagerly, joyously demanded they marry immediately.

She thought again of Farid and his impromptu proposal. A marriage in name only, undertaken to alleviate any scandal to the crown. She could never agree to such an arrangement. She'd always wanted more for herself than a loveless marriage.

Tears oozed from beneath her eyelids. She could not so easily give up her dreams of being loved by a special man, of creating the kind of family she'd been raised in…a family bred in love.

No, she would not accept Farid's offer of marriage, but she also had no idea what, exactly, she was going to do. At the moment, it seemed that all she could do was cry.

She awakened to morning light dancing in through the window and it took her several seconds to orient herself. She wasn't in her familiar bed in her room in the palace in Tamir. She was in a guest house in Montebello…pregnant and unwanted by the man she'd thought she'd loved, the man she'd thought loved her.

Amazing how quickly betrayal could transform feelings of love into something different, she thought. This morning, rather than heartache, she felt a growing edge of anger. How dare Desmond Caruso play games with her head…with her heart?

Her anger was not only directed at the man who had betrayed her, but at herself as well. How could she have been so stupid?

She sat up quickly and instantly flopped back down as a wave of nausea swept through her. It was not unfamiliar. The morning sickness had begun the week before, which had prompted her to take a pregnancy test…the test that had told her her time with Desmond had not been without consequence.

Knowing from experience that the nausea would pass in a few minutes, she simply remained still, letting her mind flow free over the events of the past twenty-four hours.

She'd always known that, as a Princess of Tamir, she might be sought out only for her position and wealth and not for herself as a woman. But she'd always believed she'd know the difference between a man who was coveting a closeness to the crown and a man who wanted to capture her heart.

Desmond had fooled her completely, and the thought of how easily she'd been fooled left a bad taste in her mouth.

Dismissing him from her mind, she focused on the room where she had slept. She'd paid little attention to it the night before, and now looked around with interest.

As with the living room, the dominant colors of the bedroom were blue and gold. Thick royal-blue curtains hung at the window, held open by braided gold tiebacks. The furniture was a light wood, graceful and unobtrusive, as if refusing to compete with the beauty of the intricately designed, sumptuous bedspread and the Oriental rug that looked far too beautiful to walk upon.

She sat up slowly, tired of the bed and of her own thoughts. She knew it was probably after ten by the cast of the sunshine from the window. The nausea was gone, so she got out of bed and padded into the bathroom.

She took a long, hot shower, luxuriating in the energizing hard spray of water, then dressed in a short-sleeved, long cotton dress. She had brought both Western and traditional Tamiri clothing with her, but opted for the simplicity of the dress.

By the time she had dressed and left her bedroom, a bit of her normal optimism had returned. Somehow, someway, she'd come up with a solution to her dilemma. All she needed was a little time.

Farid was seated on the sofa as she walked into the living room. He sprang to his feet as she entered, and she waved him back down.

"Don't you ever relax?" she asked with a sudden edge of irritation. The man looked as tightly coiled as a cobra ready to spring. Clad in his usual attire of a crisp white shirt, navy dress slacks and a suit jacket with the Tamir family crest on the pocket, there was no way he could be mistaken for anything other than what he was…a bodyguard.

"Never when I'm on duty," he replied. "Coffee and a basket of bread and rolls were delivered a little while ago. Would you like me to pour you some coffee or perhaps order something more substantial for your breakfast?"

"No, thank you." She knew better than to try coffee first thing in the morning. She was better off keeping her stomach empty until after noon.

"I made some phone calls this morning and the jet

can be readied at a moment's notice for the return trip to Tamir," he said.

"I'm not returning home today," she said and sat down on the sofa. She picked an apple from the fruit bowl in the center of the coffee table and ran her fingertips across the firm, shiny red skin.

"With all due respect, Princess, putting off the inevitable changes nothing."

She wasn't sure why, but the calm reason in his voice only served to spark another dose of irritation. "I came to Montebello for a week of vacation. I intend to stay the week...perhaps even longer."

He gave her a curt bow, his handsome features reflecting nothing. "As you wish."

She put the apple back in the bowl and gazed up at him. "You know what I really wish? I wish that for just a little while I could be a simple tourist enjoying the sights of Montebello with nothing more on my mind than what presents to bring back to my family."

She stood, far too restless to sit still. "You're right, Farid. Putting off telling my parents changes nothing, but it also doesn't hurt anything. I need some time, and I've decided we're staying."

"As you wish."

"And please stop saying that," she exclaimed fervently. "None of this is as I wish." She flushed. "I'm sorry, I didn't mean to yell."

She wasn't certain, but she thought she saw a ghost of a smile touch his lips. It was there only a moment, then gone. "With all due respect, Princess, that was a very low-key kind of yell."

The smile she thought she had seen gave her courage, and she reached out and grabbed his hands in hers. He had big, strong hands, and for a moment she wished they would close around hers, communicate to her a sense of security and well-being.

"Oh, Farid, what I want is a week of not being a princess, a week of not being a pregnant, unmarried princess who has no idea what's going to happen to her. I don't want to think of what is facing me upon my return to Tamir. I don't want a bodyguard, and I don't want attention. I just want some time to feel free, and think, and try to decide what my future will be."

He frowned and pulled his hands from hers, his dark eyes obviously troubled by her words. "I cannot permit you to wander Montebello alone. My duty is to protect you from harm and I won't shirk that duty."

Again she reached for his hands and grabbed them tightly. "I'm not asking you to let me wander alone. But don't you have other clothing, something more casual without the official Tamir royal crest? Can't you accompany me on my explorations looking like my friend and companion instead of my bodyguard?"

He looked down at the dark suit jacket he wore, the Tamir royal crest emblazoned on the breast pocket. "I only brought my official clothing with me."

She forced a bright smile. "Then we'll spend the

day shopping.'' She felt her smile falter. ''And we won't talk about what I'm going to do when I return to Tamir.''

She dropped Farid's hands, wishing the man didn't look so grim. She knew what he wanted, what he thought best was that they immediately return to Tamir and speak to her father and mother about the condition she found herself in.

But she wasn't ready to face her parents' disappointment and anger. She wasn't ready to go home and face the fact that not only would her pregnancy create a royal scandal, but it would break her parents' hearts.

Besides, before she returned home, she had to figure out how she could give her child the best possible future.

Chapter 3

The piazza just outside the gates of the Royal Palace grounds teemed with people and activity. The air was an olfactory delight, scented with the citrus smell of fresh fruit, the heavy odor of exotic spices and the savory scents that wafted from the open doors of the restaurants.

There was a cacophony of sound—merchants hawking wares, children laughing as they chased one another and adult voices greeting each other or haggling over the price of a particular item.

Farid stood just behind Samira, watching as she looked at a display of brightly colored silk scarves in one of the open markets that lined the cobblestone streets.

He felt naked without his suit coat, but Samira had insisted that he remove it before they left the guest house. He knew later, as the sun overhead grew more intense, he would be grateful to be rid of it, but at the moment he felt uncharacteristically underdressed.

''These are beautiful,'' Samira said to the man selling the scarves as she pulled money from her purse. Farid noticed how the sunlight danced on the darkness of her hair, and found himself wondering if it was as silky to the touch as it looked.

He had no doubt that she would agree to marry him despite her words to the contrary. She had no other viable alternatives. She simply needed some time to reach the realization that marriage to him was the only solution to her problem.

Without emotion or passion for one another muddying the waters, there was no reason why a marriage between them wouldn't be a success, especially since he was fairly certain the arrangement would be temporary.

Once she got back to Tamir and resumed her life as a princess, she wouldn't want to remain married to her bodyguard. But he would claim fatherhood to the child she carried and they could work together to provide the best possible life for the child without loving one another and without staying married to each other.

To the outside world, he would be the father of her child until the child was old enough to know the truth of its parentage.

He focused on the transaction taking place between Samira and the vendor.

"I'll take them both," Samira said, two scarves in her hand.

The overweight seller of scarves grinned, his over-size teeth flashing beneath his thick mustache. "A thousand blessings on you, my dear," he said as he took her money.

Samira laughed, the sound melodic and sweet. "Thank you, sir. I can use a thousand blessings," she replied.

A wave of pleasure swept through Farid. Even before he'd become her personal bodyguard, Farid had always loved the sound of Samira's laughter. It was filled with innocence and a love of life.

When he thought of Desmond Caruso, plundering her innocence for a moment's pleasure, promising her things that were nothing more than smooth lies, his blood boiled.

With the purchased scarves folded and safely tucked away in a bag, Samira rejoined Farid.

"You should have haggled with him. You probably could have gotten both scarves for the price of one," he observed.

She wrinkled her nose with displeasure. "I don't like to haggle. Besides, my mother will be pleased with the scarves," she said, then eyed him curiously. "Does your mother like pretty scarves?"

"My mother died a year ago," he said curtly.

Samira placed a hand on his arm, her beautiful brown eyes darkened with the compassion that was so much a part of her personality. "I'm so sorry, Farid."

He wasn't sure what made him more uncomfortable, the personal topic of the conversation, or the sweet empathy that flowed from her eyes and the gentle heat of her hand on his forearm.

He never discussed his background with anyone, and he didn't intend to start with the pretty pregnant princess he was responsible for. Besides, thoughts of his mother brought forth a well of conflicting emotions…love for the gentle woman who had raised him—and an intense anger for what she had done to him.

He stepped away from Samira's touch. "I'm sure your mother will be most pleased with the scarves. She's a good woman."

Farid was rewarded with a smile from Samira as her thoughts apparently turned to her own mother. "I think sometimes she makes my father nervous. She can be very outspoken at times."

They continued to walk through the busy piazza. "Yes, but she's a woman who has a reputation for wisdom and laughter."

It was odd for Farid to be walking next to her, talking to her. For the months that he had been her bodyguard, she had stayed fairly close to the palace in Tamir.

When he did accompany her to meetings, or charity functions, or simply to the homes of friends, he always remained several discreet steps behind her, and he never conversed with her on any personal level.

"My mother is a wonderful, loving woman and I've always admired the relationship she and my father have.'' Samira's eyes darkened with a hint of pain. "I'd always hoped to find a man who would love, honor and respect me as my father does my mother. I always hoped that I'd marry a man who loved me more than anything else on the earth, a man I would love the same way."

Farid said nothing, but he wondered if perhaps when they returned to Tamir she would regret telling him too much of her personal life and dreams.

After all, he was merely a servant in her life, a peasant farmer turned bodyguard, with humble beginnings. Nobody knew the secret of his birth, a secret he had learned upon his mother's death.

Their conversation about her parents had made her sad. Farid struggled to find something to say to alleviate the haunting shadows in her eyes, but before he could say anything a little girl careened into them, tears streaming down her plump little face.

"Sweetie, what's wrong?" Samira bent down on one knee, unmindful of the dusty cobblestones beneath her pale beige dress. She drew the child against her. "Why are you crying, honey?"

"I want my mommy," the little girl said amid sobs of tears.

"Is your mommy lost?" Samira asked. The child nodded her head. "Sweetheart, it's all right." She pulled the girl into her arms and gently patted her back. "We'll find your mommy for you." She looked up at Farid, beseeching him to do something.

The little girl had stopped crying and now clung to Samira as if they were new best friends. Farid reached down and plucked the child from her so she could rise from the dusty ground.

The girl's eyes widened, but she didn't cry. "Tell me, little one," he said, keeping his voice soft and gentle. "What does your mommy look like?"

"She's big. But not big like you," she said, her eyes wide and filled with misery.

Farid was conscious of Samira standing right next to him, her body heat radiating outward. The scent of her stirred his senses. He focused on the child in his arms. "And what color is her hair?"

She pointed to Samira's dark, shining hair. "Like that."

"That narrows it down," Farid muttered. Practically every woman on the piazza had dark hair.

The little girl placed a tiny hand on Farid's cheek. "You look like my daddy." Her bottom lip quivered ominously. "I want my daddy. I want my mommy." Farid looked helplessly at Samira as the girl burst into tears once again.

At that moment they heard a woman's voice frantically calling above the din of the piazza. "Tamara! Where are you, baby?"

"That's my mommy!"

"I guess she's not lost anymore. Let's go find her," Farid said and smiled at the little girl. He looked at Samira, then nodded in the direction of the woman's voice. Together they walked through the crowd to find her.

Within minutes a happy reunion had taken place between mother and child, and Samira and Farid were seated at a table in the Red Dragon Pub to enjoy some lunch.

Samira had been curiously silent since Farid had handed the young Tamara back to her grateful mother. As they'd walked along the cobblestones toward the pub, he'd felt her gaze lingering on him.

He now sat across from her, the scent of the fresh-cut floral centerpiece in the middle of the table mingling with the savory smells of browning meats and steaming vegetables. She cast him surreptitious glances above the menu she held in her hands.

He wasn't sure why, but he somehow felt as if she were judging him, taking his measure not only as a bodyguard but as a man. It set him on edge.

It wasn't until after they'd ordered that she leaned forward in her chair and gazed at him intently. "You're good with children," she said, more than a touch of surprise in her voice.

"You thought perhaps I ate children for breakfast?" He was aware of the irritation in his own voice.

Her face brightened with a blush. "Of course not. I just…I just…" Her voice trailed off and she stared into her water glass. "It surprised me, that's all."

"I like children," he said.

She sighed, and when she looked up at him again, the dark shadows of unhappiness were back in her eyes. "Desmond told me he loved children. When I told him that my heart's desire was to be a wife and a mother, he told me he'd always wanted a family."

She shook her head and once again averted her

gaze from his. "I still can't believe I was such a fool where he was concerned."

Her unhappiness not only darkened her lovely eyes, but also wafted from her, a cloud of despair that seemed to settle on his shoulders.

Again an uncharacteristic protectiveness rose inside him, and he wanted to hunt down Desmond Caruso and put enough fear in the man that he would never again take advantage of a sweet-natured, vulnerable woman.

"Princess," he began softly.

She held up a hand. "Please, at least for the time we're away from Tamir, please call me Samira."

"Samira," he said, her given name feeling strange on his lips. "As I told you last night, you don't have to face this alone. We will marry and nobody will have to know the truth about your pregnancy. Everyone will just assume the child is mine."

That is, nobody would know until the child was old enough to handle the truth. Then the truth would be told, for Farid knew more than anyone how lies, even ones of omission, could hurt and grow bitterness in the heart.

It was the smile that had made Samira reevaluate Farid. It had been the warmth of his eyes, his gentle tone and that darned smile as he'd spoken to the lost little girl.

A grim-faced, arrogant Farid was handsome, but a smiling, tender Farid was positively breathtaking. The sight had shaken her for most of the afternoon.

She now stood beneath the shower, washing off the dust from the day spent in the bustling piazza. They had eaten a silent but leisurely lunch at the Red Dragon Pub, then had shopped the rest of the afternoon.

She had insisted that Farid buy some casual clothing for the days they would remain in Montebello. She wanted nobody on the street to recognize her, and she prayed nobody would mention to Desmond that she was here in Montebello. If he didn't know already. She wasn't ready to see him, wasn't ready for any sort of confrontation with him.

All throughout the afternoon, Farid's marriage proposal had never been far from her mind. She wanted to do what was best for the child she carried, wanted to do what was best for her parents and the good of her country.

She knew accepting Farid's marriage proposal would solve a lot of problems, but there was a small part of her head...of her heart, that clung to the notion, to the promise of marrying for love.

And that was what she'd be giving up in marrying Farid.

She shut off the water and grabbed one of the thick, fluffy towels. It seemed odd not to have a maid waiting with a heated towel ready, but she had dismissed all the staff, preferring nobody around while she tried to make a decision about her situation.

The day spent with Farid had brought her no closer to making a final decision, but his surprising pronouncement that he liked children had underscored just how little she knew about the man who had proposed to her.

All she knew for certain was that he was thirty-two years old and had worked for the crown in one capacity or another since he was twenty years old.

She knew nothing of his life, of the experiences that had made him the man he was at this moment in time. And for the first time since he'd become her personal bodyguard, she wanted to know these kinds of things.

She left the bathroom and returned to the bedroom where she stood before the closet and tried to decide what to put on for a leisurely evening. She thought to spend the evening hours doing some needlework and trying to make a final decision concerning her future.

Opting for traditional rather than Western wear, Samira chose a vivid green *jalabiya* elaborately embroidered around the neck and wrists with silver thread. The material was light, almost gauzy...perfect for a balmy evening.

Beneath the *jalabiya* she wore the traditional pants, gathered at the ankles. Harem pants, as people in the Western world would describe them. For the first time since her arrival in Montebello, she wished for the presence of her personal maid, Saarah. Saarah was a sweet young woman who accomplished magic with Samira's thick hair. She brushed her hair and caught it with a large gold clip at the nape of her neck. Not exactly Saarah's magic, but adequate.

The moment she was dressed in the comfortable,

familiar clothing, a burst of homesickness swept through her. While she wasn't prepared to return home yet, she wanted—suddenly *needed*—to hear the sound of her mother's voice.

She stretched out across the bed and picked up the phone receiver on the nightstand. It took her only seconds to punch in the number that would ring her mother's private line in the Tamir palace.

Salma Hadi, Alima Kamal's favorite maid, answered the phone and a moment later Alima's strong voice filled the line. "Samira, is everything all right?"

At the sweet, loving concern in her mother's voice Samira felt tears spring to her eyes. How she hated to disappoint her mother, who had been such a well of love and support all of her life.

She swallowed hard against the tears, not wanting her mother to know she was in emotional turmoil. "And what could be wrong?" she replied with a forced lightness.

"I'm just surprised that you called. You've been away from home less than twenty-four hours." There was a pregnant pause, and Samira realized that calling her mother had probably been a mistake. Alima Kamal had unerring instincts where her children were concerned.

"Silly me, I came here to visit with Princess Anna, but when we arrived here we learned she wasn't here. She's in America."

"Then you will be returning to Tamir?" Alima asked.

"Not until later in the week. I'm going to take some time to explore the sights of Montebello. I shopped in the piazza today and bought you a present."

Alima laughed, the rich, robust laughter that had captured the heart of a sheik when she'd been a young woman. "Ah, that's one thing my three daughters have in common...their love of shopping." Her laughter faded. "Samira, are you sure everything is all right?"

"Everything is just fine. I have a lovely guest house on the palace grounds, and King Marcus and Queen Gwendolyn were quite gracious when they welcomed me."

"There must be much happiness in Montebello right now with Prince Lucas returned and with the announcement that he will be officially declared crown prince in January."

Happiness in Montebello? Samira had been too wrapped up in her own misery to notice the mood of the people of the small country. "Yes," she replied vaguely. "People seem very happy that he's well and back where he belongs."

Once again there was silence between the two women and Samira had to fight with herself not to blurt out the whole miserable truth about Desmond and her pregnancy. "Well, I'd better let you go," she said, afraid to speak to her mother any longer, afraid she might blurt out the entire horrible truth.

"Samira, you know I love you and your father loves you as well. If there's something wrong, or you're unhappy about something, you know you can come to us.''

"Of course,'' Samira replied quickly, aware that her impromptu phone call had only managed to worry her mother. "Everything is fine, really,'' she said in a last attempt to soothe her mother's concern. "I just had a few minutes and thought I would give you a quick call.''

After murmuring loving goodbyes, the two women hung up and Samira left the bedroom.

Farid stood at the window, staring outside, and the moment she entered the living room she could smell his masculine scent. It was obvious that while she had showered and changed clothes, he had done the same.

His raven hair was still damp and instead of the navy slacks and white shirt, he was clad in some of the clothes he had bought that day, a pair of casual tan slacks and a tan pullover polo shirt.

She had never seen him dressed in anything other than his uniform of dress slacks, white shirt and jacket. His official uniform had made it easy for her to think of him simply as her bodyguard.

But now, with the polo shirt stretching across his impossibly broad shoulders and the slacks riding his slender hips and clinging to his muscular thighs, she was struck by the fact that he wasn't just a formidable bodyguard, but an extremely handsome, physically appealing man as well.

He turned from the window and his gaze swept the length of her. She wondered if he found her attractive. Certainly she knew she wasn't exotic and beautiful, like her two sisters. Against her volition, she felt a blush sweep over her cheeks at her crazy thoughts.

"I just spoke with my mother," she said and sat on the sofa. Why should she care what Farid Nasir thought of her? She knew what had motivated his proposal of marriage and it had nothing to do with love or lust. It had everything to do with duty.

"All is well in Tamir?" he asked and stepped away from the window.

She nodded. "Although I think calling my mother was a mistake."

He sat in the chair opposite the sofa. "And why is that?"

Samira frowned. "My mother seems to have a sixth sense where her children are concerned. She always seems to know when something is wrong. By calling her, I think I awakened that sixth sense of hers."

"Then perhaps it's time to go back to Tamir and talk to your parents."

"I'm not ready to return yet," she said and touched her stomach reflectively. And with these words she also realized she was not yet ready to give up on her dreams of marrying for love.

The path she chose to walk suddenly became clear to her. "I need to stay here for a little longer. I need to get strong."

One of his dark eyebrows quirked upward. "Strong?"

She nodded and stood, unable to sit while her mind worked to become comfortable with the decision she'd made in the past few moments. "I'm not exactly the rebellious type," she said as she paced across the exquisite Oriental rug beneath her feet. "I've always been the daughter who gave my parents no grief, who always abided by their wishes and tried to please them."

For the second time in the past twenty-four hours she thought she saw a whisper of a smile curve the corners of his lips. "For as long as I have worked at the palace, from all the gossip and reports I've ever heard, you have been a good and dutiful daughter."

She tore her gaze from him, finding the hint of the smile that touched his full, sensual lips far too appealing. How would those sensual lips feel pressed against her own? She shook her head to dispel the image and focused on the conversation at hand.

"Yes," she agreed. "I've always been a dutiful daughter and I've never rocked the boat in any way. But now I must choose a path that is right for me and the child I carry. Somehow I have to become strong enough to resist my father. I know he'll try to get me to tell him the name of the father, but I won't." She looked at him once again. "And you must promise me that you won't tell him, either."

She could tell by the grim expression on his face that he didn't want to agree to what she'd asked. "If we marry, then there's no reason for your father to question who the father of your child is," he countered. "It will be implied that the child is mine."

"I'm not going to marry you, Farid," she exclaimed. "And I'm not going to let my father force me into marriage with any other man. I've decided not to marry anyone." She raised her chin another notch. "I'm perfectly capable of raising my baby alone."

Farid stood, his eyes darkened by deep disapproval. "That is the most ridiculous thing I've ever heard in my life," he exclaimed, his voice radiating an anger she'd never heard there before, an anger that seemed to have sprung from thin air.

She stared at him in stunned surprise. "Excuse me?"

"You heard me," he replied curtly. He drew a deep breath, as if to steady himself, and Samira sank back down on the sofa, shocked by his unexpected, impassioned reaction to her announcement.

"I thought this was all settled," he continued, "that we would agree to have a marriage in name only and that would solve everything."

"Then you thought wrong," Samira replied with a rising anger of her own.

What did he think? That she wasn't capable of raising a child by herself? Was he afraid that somehow she couldn't be a good mother? That she was incompetent? "Nothing was settled, and I told you last night that marriage to you wasn't a solution."

"I know what you said last night, but I thought you needed some time to get used to the idea." The lips she'd thought so sensual-looking before were now a slash of grimness, and his eyes were cold depths of darkness.

"I have agreed to be your husband so you can save face with your parents, with your countrymen. There will be a little gossip because I was your bodyguard, but certainly not to the extent that there will be if you don't marry at all and bear a child out of wedlock.'' His dark gaze bore into hers. ''You have few alternatives.''

''I don't care about gossip and I don't need you,'' she retorted.

''Yes, you do,'' he countered. He walked to stand directly over her, and she had the feeling he was subtly trying to intimidate her.

''You yourself said that there is no other man in your life, and few men would be willing to step in and raise a child who is not their own,'' he exclaimed.

''That doesn't mean that I'm positively desperate to accept your marriage proposition,'' she exclaimed. She raised her chin defiantly, refusing to be intimidated either by his hulking nearness or the harsh glare of his eyes.

''You should be desperate to accept, if not for yourself, then for your baby. Children need fathers, and you are being selfish if you deny your child that.''

Despite her wishes to the contrary, his last words struck home. She frowned and eyed him for a long moment. ''What about love?'' she asked in a small voice. ''Isn't that important, too?''

He snorted in obvious disgust. ''Giving your child a father is what's important. It's time to put away your foolish dreams of silly, romantic love and make the best possible decision for the child you carry. Besides, isn't it your silly notion about love that got you in this predicament?''

She gasped, appalled by his words and the hateful reminder of her own stupidity. She jumped up off the sofa and shoved past him, unsure if it was anger or hurt that tightened painfully in her chest.

She clung to the anger. ''I am thinking about the child I carry,'' she said, even more angered when tears filled her eyes. ''Why on earth would I subject my child to a father like you? A cold, arrogant man who believes love is nothing more than a foolish dream?''

She didn't wait for him to reply, but instead ran into the bedroom and slammed the door behind her.

Chapter 4

Farid stared at the closed bedroom door and realized he'd been out of line...way out of line. He had spoken to her not as a servant, but as an equal. He'd practically yelled at her, and that was unacceptable behavior.

He hadn't realized until this moment how much he had embraced the idea of stepping into Samira's life as helpmate and father to her unborn child. He'd been well aware of the fact that a marriage to Samira would in all likelihood be temporary, but the commitment he made to her child would last a lifetime.

Certainly it was duty that drove him—duty and the desire to honor a promise to a dead man, but it was also more than that.

He knew what it was like to grow up with an aching need inside, the need for a father. He didn't want

Samira's child to grow up with that same sense of emptiness.

In his case, the emptiness could have been filled had his mother only told him the truth. But she hadn't. She hadn't told him the truth until it was far too late. He shoved the thought away, hating the anger that instantly pressed tight against his chest.

Swiping a hand through his hair, he walked over to the window and stared out at the manicured gardens in the distance. For a moment, as he'd faced off with her, he'd forgotten that she was a princess and he was merely her servant.

He'd forgotten everything except the fact that if she didn't marry him, she would be fodder for gossip and the child she bore would be branded a fatherless bastard. He'd forgotten everything except his own need to make sure that her child didn't suffer the same kind of empty childhood *he* had.

He owed her an apology, but apologies had never come easily to Farid. He moved away from the window and sat, deciding he'd wait until she came out of the bedroom to make an apology to her.

As he waited, he thought over the events of the day. She had been quiet throughout the afternoon of shopping. After lunch they had wandered the piazza, going in and out of the little shops along the way.

She had bought presents not only for her family members, but for friends and favorite servants as well, and he was reminded again that Samira was known for her generous nature. And it was the generosity of her nature and her spirit that made her a favorite among the royal family.

Farid knew there were many who sought out Samira's advice when it came to matters of the heart. Apparently there were some who appreciated her fanciful notion of love.

One thing was clear to him. She was right when she'd said she'd always been the dutiful daughter who had never caused her parents any grief. Of the princesses of Tamir, Samira had always been the quietest, the most unassuming of the three.

She spent much of her time involved in a variety of charity work and was a major supporter, both financially and emotionally, of promoting literacy in Tamir.

He had a feeling she would never be strong enough to stand up to her father no matter how much time she spent here preparing to do so.

She remained in her room until dusk had fallen outside, then she swept out of the bedroom, her gaze not meeting his. "I'm going for a walk," she said coolly. "I need some fresh air to clear my head."

She didn't wait for him to acknowledge her words, but instead strode to the door and stepped out into the shadows of approaching night.

Farid hurried after her. "Princess Samira," he said softly, intentionally using her title to remind himself of his position. "I owe you an apology," he said.

She stopped walking and turned to face him, her expression more solemn than he'd ever seen it. "I think we owe each other an apology," she said with a graciousness he couldn't help but admire. "Please, let's just walk in the garden. I really do need some time to think." He nodded and fell in step beside her.

Landscaping lanterns softly illuminated the narrow path that wound through the formal gardens, and the air was heavily perfumed by the variety of lush flowers. The sound of a fountain bubbled from somewhere nearby, adding to the peaceful serenity of the garden.

The moon was full in the sky, spilling down a shining light that caught and reflected on the silvery threads in Samira's clothing. It made it appear as if she were covered with tiny stars.

They walked at a leisurely pace that should have been relaxing, but the thought of their heated exchange weighed heavy on Farid's shoulders.

"Do you really think I can't be a good mother?" she finally asked, breaking the silence that had lingered thickly between them as they walked.

Farid looked at her in surprise. "Of course not. In fact, I'm certain you will be a good mother."

She stopped walking and motioned to a nearby concrete bench. They sat side-by-side and she gazed at him, a little wrinkle of worry between her delicate brows. "But you don't think I'm capable of raising a child alone?"

He sighed, realizing she'd apparently misunderstood what he'd been trying to say to her during their exchange earlier. "Princess, there is no doubt in my mind that you are more than capable of raising a child by yourself, but no matter how good a mother is…a mother isn't a father. In any case, it was not my place to say those things to you. I was way out of line.''

"Apology accepted," she replied, then smiled. "And I'm sorry for calling you cold and arrogant."

"I must confess, you aren't the first to use those kinds of terms when describing me."

She smiled again, but the smile was only fleeting. She raised her face toward the moon and sighed. Farid watched her, noting how the bewitching moonlight emphasized the delicacy of her facial features.

With her head tilted back, he could see the graceful column of her throat. Her skin looked unbelievably smooth, and his fingers tingled with the sudden desire to reach out and touch.

Her eyelashes were sinfully long and thick around her almond-shaped eyes and as he watched she closed them and once again released a tiny sigh.

The sigh moved something inside him. It sounded so forlorn, so lonely. Farid knew all about loneliness. He'd lived with it for most of his life. It felt comfortable to him, but apparently not to her.

She lowered her face, opened her eyes and gazed at the grounds around them. "It's beautiful here, isn't it?"

Farid followed her example and looked around. "The gardens are impressive, but no more so than the ones in Tamir," he replied.

She smiled at him, the gesture as always filling her features with a pleasing warmth. "You're a loyal countryman." Her smile disappeared and she continued to study him. "I know so little about you, Farid. Tell me about yourself."

"What do you want to know?"

"I don't know…let's start with where you grew up."

"My parents were simple farmers and we had a little place just outside of the palace gates. I still own it, but I'm not there often." It had been difficult, going back to that place after his mother's death a year ago. There had been too many memories, both good and bad.

Once again she looked up at the moon. "I used to dream of what it would be like to be raised on a farm by an ordinary family."

Farid wondered if it was the surrounding flowers that filled his senses with such a delicious fragrance or if it was the scent of the woman seated next to him. "I thought all little girls dreamed of being princesses."

She laughed and looked at him once again. "I guess they do…unless they are a princess." She stood. "Let's walk a little more."

They walked for a few minutes in silence. This time the silence was a companionable one rather than the tense quiet that had existed between them when they'd initially left the guest house.

"I always thought life as a farmer's daughter would be far easier than life as a sheik's daughter," she finally said. "As a princess, you learn very early that people will pretend to like you because of your title, that people will try to take advantage of you for power, or position, or political reasons."

Her features tightened and her hands clenched at her sides and Farid knew what she was probably thinking. "Do you think that's what happened with Caruso?" he asked softly. "That he used you?"

"Of course that's what happened," she said, her voice holding an angry edge. "I'm not sure what he hoped to gain by seducing me, but it certainly didn't have anything to do with love."

"But you loved him?"

She didn't answer for a long moment. "No, I didn't love him. Oh, I thought I did at the time, but I realize now I was in love with the idea that he loved me. I was in love with the future he painted with his smooth, lying words."

She paused a moment to lean over a bush that held bright orange blossoms as big as a dinner plate. She breathed deeply of one of the blossoms, then turned back to him, her gaze once again curious.

"Have you ever been in love, Farid?"

"No."

She straightened, still looking at him. "There's never been a special woman in your life? Have you really never felt a kind of fluttery, valentines-and-flowers kind of love?"

"Never. To be honest, there's been little time for women. I've worked hard to achieve my position as bodyguard and that has left little time for other pursuits. Besides, the only kind of love I really believe in is the love of my country. I don't believe in that valentine-and-flower sort of love you spoke of.''

He could tell that his words disturbed her, but he couldn't pretend to be somebody he was not...not even for a princess.

Besides, if she did eventually agree to marry him, then she should know up-front that the romantic kind of love she apparently believed in would not be an option.

They continued walking. ''What about your parents? Did you love them?''

''Of course,'' he replied automatically.

''Tell me about them.''

''My mother was a simple woman. Her pleasures came from her family and from the farm. She loved planting and watching things grow and taking care of me and my father.''

''And your father?''

He frowned thoughtfully. ''My father was a good, patient man. He had a strong work ethic and a huge heart. He died when I was twelve.'' Grief welled up inside him as he thought of the man he had loved and lost. He quickly tamped it down, along with the anger that always accompanied it.

He was grateful that she didn't attempt to console or placate him with words or a touch. ''So, you know what it's like to be without a father.''

''I do.''

''And that's why you said all the things that you did to me?''

He nodded. "Every child, whether a girl or a boy, deserves the love of two parents."

Her soft brown eyes studied him for a long moment. "And you could love a child who wasn't of your blood?"

Although she asked the question with a lightness of tone, he knew his answer was vitally important. And the answer was easy. "Yes, I could easily love a child that wasn't mine, especially if I was in his or her life from the very beginning."

She nodded, her expression thoughtful. "Let's go back to the guest house. It's been a long day and I'm getting tired."

They changed direction and headed back the way they had come. She once again fell silent and the only sounds were of the insects chirping their night songs and the faint swish of her *jalabiya* against her thin pants.

"If I agreed to a marriage in name only to you, then you would be agreeing to a lifetime of celibacy." Even in the semidarkness he could see the pretty blush that accompanied her words.

"Would you not be agreeing to the same?" he countered pointedly.

"Of course..." Again that endearing little wrinkle appeared in the center of her brow and her cheeks deepened in hue with a new blush. "But, I think that sort of thing is easier for women than men."

"I don't know about other men, but if we marry, then I'll abide by the conditions you wish. I'm the master of my emotions. My emotions never rule me."

She offered him a small, teasing smile. "I think I could have guessed that."

They reentered the guest house and she turned to face him. The wrinkle across her forehead was gone and from her eyes radiated a peace he hadn't seen since they had arrived in Montebello.

"Does your marriage proposal still stand?" she asked.

He nodded, his heart suddenly quickening its pace. "Then I accept," she said. "We'll discuss the details tomorrow," she said, then turned and headed for her bedroom door. When she reached the door she turned back to look at him.

"Farid, the kind of love I once dreamed of, the valentines-and-flowers kind of love, is not a foolish or silly notion." Her eyes darkened. "It's just apparently not destined for me." She disappeared into her room.

Ursula Chambers watched Desmond Caruso from across the table in the Glass Swan Restaurant. God, the man was so hot. He was easily the best-looking man in the place with his raven-dark hair, piercing black eyes, chiseled features and charming cleft chin.

She wasn't oblivious to the admiring glances he'd received from the other female diners from the moment they'd walked into the elegant dining establishment. The fact that other women coveted him and she was the one with him filled her with an intoxicating feeling of power.

From the moment she had met him at her family

ranch in Shady Rock, Colorado, she'd known the unbelievably handsome man with royal ties just might
be her ticket to her big break in life.

"You're looking quite smug," he now said to her
as they lingered over dessert and coffee.

She smiled. "And why shouldn't I? I've just had
an incredible meal in a beautiful restaurant with a
stunning view." She swept her hand toward the window that offered a panoramic view of the harbor.

"I noticed you made sure you ordered the most
expensive items on the menu," Desmond said dryly.

"And I'm worth every dime," she replied.

"Of course you are, my love," he replied
smoothly, his dark gaze inscrutable as he looked at
her.

She wrapped her fingers around her coffee cup, her
gaze lingering on him. She was more than a little bit
in love with him and there was a part of her that felt
he had been brought into her life by the divine hand
of fate.

"What?" He looked at her expectantly.

"I was just thinking that it must have been fate
that brought us together. I mean, of all the places in
Colorado for Prince Lucas to show up after his plane
crash, he came to work on my sister's place. And then
you showed up looking for clues to his whereabouts."

"You know how anxious we all were to find out
anything we could about Prince Lucas's well-being."
He cast a quick glance around as if to make certain
nobody else could hear their conversation.

Ursula smiled knowingly. She knew exactly what

Desmond had had in mind when he'd shown up at her ranch looking for the whereabouts of the missing heir.

If Prince Lucas wound up dead, then Desmond's half brother Lorenzo would ascend to the throne and Desmond would be assured a position of power.

"But now he's back. I assume he's no longer suffering any amnesia?"

"No. It appears he has all his memories back." Desmond frowned, the gesture doing nothing to detract from his attractiveness. "Which, unfortunately, means he remembers that he's never particularly liked me."

Ursula ran a perfectly manicured index finger around the rim of her coffee cup, then looked up at him once again. "Don't worry, Desmond, I have the means to see to it that Prince Lucas is forever in your debt…and mine." She saw the sharp edge of hunger that lit his eyes, the intensity that suddenly radiated from his body.

"What is it, Ursula?" He leaned across the table and she could smell the woodsy scent of his expensive cologne. "Tell me what you know."

He reached across the table and took one of her hands in his. As always, she thrilled at his touch.

Damn him. She wanted to see that hunger in his eyes for her, not for what secrets he thought she possessed. "Talk to me, Ursula," he urged.

Suddenly she was mad at him all over again. After all they had shared, after all their schemes and dreams, the moment the crown prince had been found and Desmond had returned to Montebello, he'd stopped communicating with her, had ignored her messages and calls.

She pulled her hand from his and rose gracefully from her chair. "I really don't think this is the time or the place. Besides, I need to go visit the ladies' room."

As she walked to the back of the restaurant toward the restrooms, she was aware of several men's gazes following her progress.

She'd once had a lover tell her she had the grace and posture of a queen with just enough sensual sway to her hips to hint at a whore.

He'd had no idea how many hours she'd practiced her walk, her stance, the very presence she radiated. He'd had no idea the sacrifices she'd made to make certain she looked as good as possible.

The continuous dieting, the exercise, the facials and hairdressers, they had all been necessities to prepare her for her glorious future…a future that was now just at the tips of her fingers.

All the bad breaks were behind her now. She was on the verge of achieving her greatest success—a permanent position of power in the Montebello palace. She would live like a queen, all thanks to her sister and the secret that burned in Ursula's heart.

The powder room in the Glass Swan was as elegant as the restaurant itself. Several gold-brocade chaise lounges awaited weary ladies and the walls were lined with brightly lit mirrors. She stood before one of the mirrors and eyed her reflection.

She'd been right in buying the little black dress she wore, although it had been prohibitively expensive. It fit her as if it had been made specifically for her, emphasizing the breasts that had cost her a small fortune, her slender waistline and slim hips.

The darkness of the dress enhanced the blond of her hair and the blue of her eyes. Leaning closer to the mirror, she frowned as she saw the tiny lines that fanned out from her eyes.

She was thirty-five years old and it was beginning to show. A terrified desperation swept through her, along with a rage at the unfairness of life.

She'd always believed that by the time she reached thirty she'd be a famous, wealthy actress. She'd gone to New York City with that goal in mind and had hooked up with a manager who'd quickly become her lover.

Unfortunately, Derek had dropped her not only as a lover, but as a client, and her dreams of power and prestige had gone up in smoke. She'd been forced to run back to the ranch in Colorado with her tail tucked between her legs.

She withdrew a tube of lipstick from her purse and slid the scarlet color across her lips. But now she had the biggest role of her life ahead of her, the role that would see all her dreams come true. She'd even orchestrated the murder of her sister for the plum role of a lifetime.

She twisted the lipstick back into its tube and dropped it back into her purse. Poor Jessica. She'd fallen in love with a ranch hand, not knowing he was a prince suffering from amnesia. And when she'd discovered herself pregnant with the prince's child, she'd refused to use the child as a pawn.

Stupid, pathetic Jessica. She hadn't realized the power the child represented. She'd had to be sacrificed for the sake of Ursula's future.

Now all the pieces of that future were in a line and all she needed was a little more capital and a little grease to see things through. The money she'd gotten from selling her sister's heirloom ring wouldn't last forever. And that's where Desmond came into the plan.

Of course, what she hoped was that Desmond would marry her, and together with the child they would wield more power than anyone else in the palace.

Again she felt a stir of anger coupled with the ugly taste of despair as she thought of Desmond refusing her calls and messages since she'd been in Montebello.

She couldn't believe that he'd just decided to roll over and play dead…given up on the idea of having any sort of power or influence with the royalty of Montebello. Desmond wasn't the kind to just give up. So what was going on with him? And why had he been avoiding her?

She left the restroom and went back the table where Desmond had apparently already paid for their meal and was ready to leave.

He pulled her close to him as they walked out of

the restaurant. "I thought we could go back to your hotel room. We can talk in private there."

"No, let's go to your place," she countered. "And before I tell you anything, Desmond, I want you to make love to me. I want you to show me just how much you've missed me."

His gaze bore into hers, breathtakingly intense. "You know I want that as much as you do, darling. I've missed making love to you." He leaned down and nibbled the skin just below her ear.

A thrill rushed through her at his words and a shiver worked up her spine as his lips danced erotically down her neck.

Maybe he did care for her more than just a little. Still, she wasn't letting him off the hook so easily.

Maybe after they made love, she'd tell him what she knew. But, then again…maybe she wouldn't.

Chapter 5

"I've thought it over carefully," Samira said to Farid the next afternoon. They were in a little restaurant called the Sultan's Den, having a late lunch.

Samira had slept sinfully late after a night of restless tossing and turning. Sleep had been long in coming as she'd struggled with doubts about the decision she'd made concerning not only her own future, but that of the child she carried as well.

"I think we should marry immediately, right here in Montebello," she said.

Farid raised a dark brow. Again today he was dressed in casual clothing. Navy slacks hugged his slender hips and a short-sleeved pale blue and navy striped shirt exposed his muscular biceps and forearms.

"We can remarry with my family members present

once we return to Tamir,'' she hurriedly added. ''But I think we should spend a couple of weeks here... married...to get better acquainted and more at ease with one another. Otherwise my parents won't believe that we've been...uh...lovers for the past three months.''

She looked down at her salad, unable to maintain eye contact with him as she talked of them being lovers. Would Farid be a good lover? She shoved the thought aside, knowing it was foolish to even entertain the notion. They were agreeing to a marriage in name only, one that would preclude any physical contact.

''Don't you think it would be better to marry in Tamir with your mother and father's blessing?'' Although his tone was even, she sensed his disapproval with what she had planned.

He didn't understand her fear—the fear that if she returned to Tamir without already being married to Farid, she would crumble beneath her father's questions and tell the truth about Desmond Caruso.

She was frightened that she wasn't strong enough to stand up to her father and choose her own path. But here in Montebello at this very moment in time, she was strong enough to choose her destiny—a destiny void of love, but one of dignity.

''I think it's better if we do it as I've planned.'' She looked up at him again, grateful to see none of the disapproval she'd thought she'd heard in his voice on his features.

"Won't your parents find it odd that you're staying so long here in Tamir?" he asked.

She used her fork to toy with a piece of lettuce. "I'll tell them I'm awaiting Princess Anna's return from the States. There is nothing pressing on my calendar for the next couple of weeks and no reason for me to hurry back to Tamir. They probably won't question my decision to remain here for a while."

Farid shoved his empty plate aside and instead wrapped his large hands around a steaming mug of coffee. "And how will we accomplish this wedding here in Montebello?"

Samira took a sip of her water, once again fighting any doubts that might flitter through her mind concerning her choice in marrying Farid.

She had to focus on the fact that she knew he would be a good husband, and more important, a good father to the baby she carried. She couldn't forget how good he'd been with the lost little girl in the piazza.

"There's an old family friend living here in Montebello. His name is Abdul Geta, and he's the Imam in a small mosque east of here. He would marry us."

"Without your father's permission?" Farid asked.

Samira smiled as she thought of her old teacher. "Abdul and my father were longtime friends. Six months ago they had a fight and Abdul left Tamir in a temper fit, claiming my father was the most stubborn, irritating, thickheaded man he'd ever known. I think Abdul will be pleased to marry us without my father's consent."

Farid took a sip of his coffee. As always, his expression was inscrutable. "When you say you wish us to marry immediately, exactly when are you talking about?"

"Today." Now that she'd made her decision, she wanted the marriage to take place as soon as possible. "I thought this afternoon we could drive out to find Abdul." She set her fork down next to her plate. "And I think it best that we keep our marriage a secret until we are ready to return to Tamir."

He looked down into his coffee cup, a frown drawing his eyebrows closer together in the center of his brow. It was obvious he was contemplating the pros and cons of what she was suggesting.

"You trust this Abdul?" he finally asked.

She nodded. "With my life. Abdul and I had a special relationship." She thought of the hours she and the old scholar had talked, exchanging ideas on everything from religion to computer games. He had been like a favorite, beloved uncle to her, and she'd missed him since he'd left Tamir.

Farid sipped his coffee once again, the thoughtful wrinkle deepening in the center of his forehead. "We'll need to rent a car. If you wish to keep this a secret, then we don't want to have one of the palace vehicles take us to Abdul. That would draw unwanted attention to us."

"I agree." She was grateful he was going along with her plans. "A rental car would be best." She took another sip of her water. All the talk of marriage and subterfuge was making her mouth unaccountably dry.

She looked at the man across from her, the man who had agreed to step up to protect her and her family from gossip. He was so handsome, with his rich olive complexion and large dark eyes. His handsomeness was far different from Desmond Caruso's, although no less compelling.

Desmond's eyes hadn't held the same liquid depths that Farid's did. Desmond's chiseled features had not held the quiet strength found in the sculptured planes and square jaw of Farid's face.

He could easily have chosen a beautiful woman as his wife, and had a marriage based on passion rather than a marriage based on duty.

"Farid, are you sure you want to do this?" she asked. She eyed him worriedly. She had no idea what she'd do if he changed his mind, but would never pressure him to go through with the marriage.

He smiled at her, the first open, honest smile she'd ever seen. The gesture shot warmth into his dark eyes, curved his sensual full lips upward and created starbursts of appealing smile lines at the corners of his eyes. "Don't worry, Samira. There are no doubts in my mind. If it's what you wish, then I would be honored to become your husband and the father to your child."

The smile, coupled with the words she so desperately wanted to hear, sent a burst of gratitude and sudden affection through her. "I will see to it that my father rewards you handsomely."

"My reward is knowing that I'm doing what's right for my country."

His words were a harsh reminder to Samira. She had to remember that Farid was a man of duty and that seemed to be the sum of him.

She placed her napkin next to her plate. "Shall we go back to the guest house and arrange for a car?"

He nodded, and within half an hour they were back in the guest house. While Farid arranged for a car to meet them outside the palace gates, Samira called her mother to tell her they were staying longer than they'd initially planned.

Thankfully, Alima accepted her daughter's explanation without question. After hanging up the phone, Samira eyed the clothing she had brought with her to Montebello and tried to decide what would be appropriate wedding attire.

Her wedding.

For a moment, as she stood before the closet, she closed her eyes and thought of the wedding dreams she'd entertained for as long as she could remember.

She'd always believed that she would marry in a ceremony with her parents present and proud, with her sisters and brothers surrounding her, and that she would be binding her life to a man she loved above all others.

As a young woman she'd fantasized about her wedding night, a night of unbridled passion coupled with sweet murmurs of love forever.

She opened her eyes and placed her hands over her lower abdomen. It was time to put away her girlish dreams, time to grow up and realize that the kind of love she'd once dreamed about was to be sacrificed for the welfare of the baby she carried.

Still, she only intended to be married once in her life, so she wanted to wear something special. She finally settled on a gauzy, off-white dress that she'd never worn before and that probably wouldn't wrinkle during the hour or two ride in the car.

After she'd slipped on the dress, she stared at her reflection in the bathroom mirror. She was about to marry a man she didn't love, a man who had made it fairly clear he didn't even believe in love…at least not the kind of love she'd always dreamed about.

She steadfastly refused to consider whether it was the right thing to do or not. She'd made her decision, and as far as she was concerned, she had only one choice that made any kind of sense—to marry her bodyguard.

It had been a while since Farid had been behind the steering wheel of a car, and with each mile that passed, he remembered how much he enjoyed driving.

Most of the time, whenever the princess went anywhere, a car and driver were provided and Farid always rode with her. He cast a surreptitious glance at the woman seated next to him.

It touched him that she'd changed clothes, that even though they were entering into a relationship more like a legal contract than a marriage, it had been important enough to her that she'd dressed up.

He tried not to notice the thrust of her breasts against the bodice of the thin dress and attempted to ignore the heady scent of her that filled the confines of the car.

"Beautiful country, isn't it?" he asked in an attempt to alleviate the silence that had prevailed between them during the drive.

"It reminds me of Tamir," she replied. "It has the same beautiful beaches and soaring mountains."

That seemed to exhaust the conversation about the geological delights of Montebello, and again they both fell silent.

Farid wondered if she was entertaining second thoughts about the marriage. He entertained none. He'd been assigned to protect Samira. Of course, the best thing that could have happened would have been for Desmond Caruso to be a good and decent man. He and Samira would have married and raised their child together.

But Farid would not see her married to a man like Caruso. His princess deserved better, and Farid vowed to be a good husband to the princess he was sworn to protect. He would stay with her for as long as she wanted him to, and when she decided it was time for their marriage to end, he would step away from her life with dignity and honor.

"Samira, you realize that no matter what happens in the future between us, I will always want to be a part of your child's life."

"You sound as if you have little hope of a marriage between us lasting for any length of time."

He shrugged. "I just want you to understand that I will be a father to your child for as long as you want me to be."

"I already knew that, Farid," she said softly. "It's one of the reasons I've decided to go forward with this." She turned her attention back out the window.

"What was the name of the town where Abdul lives?" he asked when they'd been driving for a little over an hour.

"Kyrna," she replied. She pulled the map from the glove box and opened it. "It should be the next town we come to. I can't wait to see Abdul and his family again."

Within minutes they were in the small town of Kyrna and had located the small but well-tended mosque. Several young boys sat on the grass surrounding the traditional fountain in the center courtyard in front of the place of worship.

"We're looking for the Imam," Farid said to the boys as he and Samira approached the mosque. The Imam was the leader of the mosque. "Abdul Geta?"

"He's not here," one of the boys replied. "He's at home this time of the day."

"And where is his home?" Samira asked.

A younger boy pointed toward a nearby street. "Down that way, three houses on the left."

"Thank you," Farid said and the two of them once again got back into the car. He drove to the house where the boy had indicated Abdul Geta lived, then put the car into Park and turned to look at Samira.

He could see a pulse beating in the hollow of her

throat. It made her look achingly vulnerable, and more than a little frightened.

"You know it isn't too late to change your mind about all this," he said softly.

Her eyes widened slightly. "Have you changed your mind?"

"No, Samira. I haven't changed my mind, but I want you to understand that if you do, there will be no hard feelings."

The smile she offered him lit a small flame in the pit of his stomach. "Good, because I don't believe in harboring hard feelings. Life is far too short." She opened her car door. "Shall we go find Abdul?"

Yes, Farid thought as he followed her to the entrance of the house. Samira wasn't the type to hold a grudge against anyone. Unlike Farid.

The door was answered by an old man wearing a traditional *dishdashah*. The long white cotton dress looked oddly elegant on his thin, tall frame. He uttered a nonsensical sound of surprise, then grabbed Samira and hugged her to his chest.

"Ah, my little one," he exclaimed, his affection for the princess obvious. "How good it is to see you. Come, come into my humble home." He gestured both of them inside, where the living room was dark and cool and the air smelled of something spicy cooking.

Samira introduced the two men. Together she and Farid sat on the sofa while Abdul took the chair directly across from them.

"Ah, Samira, I have missed you," he said, his dark

eyes lit with obvious affection. "Tell me of things in Tamir…your family is well?"

For the next few minutes Samira and Abdul visited about mutual old friends and her family members. They spoke of politics and of Samira's brother's wedding.

"I would love to think that you have traveled all this way just to visit an old teacher and friend, but I sense there is more to your visit than that." Abdul gazed at Samira with unabashed curiosity.

Samira nodded. "We wish you to marry us…here… and now."

Abdul sat back in his chair and eyed them in surprise. "And why would you not marry in Tamir with your family in attendance?"

Farid kept silent, unsure how much of the truth Samira was willing to tell Abdul. To his surprise, Samira told him the entire truth…about her brief affair, the discovery of her pregnancy and Farid's offer to be both husband to her and father to her unborn child. What she didn't tell Abdul was the name of the man she'd had the affair with.

She also told him she wanted the ceremony to remain a secret until she told her parents upon their return to Tamir.

Abdul sat silently, nodding his head occasionally as Samira spoke. "Please, Abdul, you must do this for me…for us," she finished, her eyes echoing her heartfelt appeal.

When she finished, he templed his fingers on his lap and gazed at them both thoughtfully. "Marriage is not something you enter into lightly. It is a sacred bond, a joining of souls.''

"We are both committed to getting married,'' Samira replied. "We are not taking any of this lightly. We feel a union between the two of us would be a good thing.''

Abdul turned his gaze to Farid. "And you can provide for Princess Samira and the child she will have?''

"Yes, I can,'' Farid replied, although he knew he would never be able to provide Samira with the kind of lifestyle she was accustomed to having.

"And you can love the child she carries as your own?''

Farid nodded. "I can.''

Abdul stared at him for a long moment, then he nodded almost imperceptibly. "Although it isn't mandatory, I recommend not only a written marriage contract, but also a prenuptial agreement as well.''

Abdul returned his gaze to Samira. "A prenuptial agreement will protect your assets in case there is a divorce.''

"That's really not necessary,'' Samira protested. "I have no intention of getting divorced. Besides, I trust Farid completely.''

"If you draw one up, I'll sign it,'' Farid said.

"Very well.'' Abdul stood. "I have the necessary paperwork in the other room. I'll just go get it and we can have my wife and son be witnesses.''

"You don't have to sign a prenuptial agreement,'' Samira said to him once Abdul had left them alone in the room. "If I didn't trust you, I wouldn't be marrying you."

"I appreciate that, Samira, but signing a prenup is a smart thing to do."

"I have no intention of ever getting a divorce," she repeated and her eyes held an appeal, a need to hear the same sentiment from him. He didn't disappoint her.

"Nor do I," he replied. "I am in this for life, Samira." He meant it. He would not be the one to ever seek a divorce. However, he knew there was a strong possibility that when they returned to Tamir, she would.

This marriage was agreeable to her now because she was afraid of her parents, afraid to go home without being married. Once she returned to her home and to her life as a princess, Farid didn't expect the marriage to last. He was already prepared for the end before the marriage had even officially begun.

She would meet a man her equal, a man who could give her the hearts-and-flowers kind of love that she obviously believed in. A love he didn't believe in.

However, no matter how long or short the marriage, to the outside world, the child she carried would be Farid's, and he would be in the child's life for as long as he was wanted and needed.

Both Samira and Farid stood as Abdul reentered the room, this time flanked by a tall young man who resembled him and a short, squat woman with graying hair. Abdul introduced the two to Farid as Aziz, his eldest son, and Iraina, his wife.

"I have typed up a brief prenup." He handed a copy to Farid and a copy to Samira. It was brief, merely stating that each would leave the marriage with the same assets they had when they entered into the marriage. "If you'll both sign my copy, then we can proceed with the ceremony."

The ceremony to make Farid and Samira husband and wife was a short, simple one. They pronounced their desire to marry each other, then Farid was required to give Mahr. Mahr was a gift from the groom to the bride, and Farid had come prepared for such an offering.

He withdrew from his pocket a thin gold ring and handed it to Abdul. "It was my mother's ring," he said. She had given it to him days before she'd died, telling him to find love and to use the ring to symbolize that love.

It was also at that time that she'd told him the secret she'd carried for years, a secret that had ripped apart the fabric of his life and had filled him with an anger he'd yet to resolve.

But there was no place for anger in him at the moment, and he shoved away thoughts of his mother and her deception as Abdul proclaimed them husband and wife.

"And you may kiss the bride," Iraina exclaimed with a girlish giggle.

Abdul rolled his eyes. "I fear that western influences have corrupted my wife."

"But that's one of the nicer western traditions,"

Samira said and looked at Farid shyly. "I would not be averse to a kiss from my new husband."

A surge of energy swept through him, an energy that brought with it a rush of heat. Kiss Samira? In the brief time he'd had to contemplate marriage to her, he'd envisioned the two of them making parenting decisions, attending social and business meetings as a couple, and sharing a living space. He hadn't thought about kissing her.

Iraina giggled and both Abdul and his son looked at Farid in commiseration, as if to acknowledge that it was easier to bow to the wishes of their women than to fight them.

Farid stepped closer to Samira and placed his hands on her shoulders. Her eyes shone and she parted her lips slightly. He was suddenly struck with a desire so intense it half blinded him.

He didn't want to just kiss her. He wanted to slowly remove her dress and taste every inch of her silky, sweet skin. He wanted to cup her bare breasts in his hands and rub his thumbs across the peaks until she cried out his name with urgent need.

Stunned by his own thoughts, he quickly shoved them away, touched his lips to hers, then stepped back from her. He thought he saw a touch of disappointment in her eyes at the brevity of the kiss, but it was there only a moment, then gone.

They remained in Abdul's home long enough for his wife to serve them refreshments, then they got back in the rental car for the long drive back to the palace.

"What did Abdul and your father fight about that caused the rift between them?" Farid asked, seeking any kind of conversation so they wouldn't suffer an uncomfortable silence.

Married. They were married. The enormity of what they'd just done hadn't sunk in yet. He wondered later if he'd have regrets or not.

"I don't know. I remember at the time my mother said it was nothing more than male foolishness. Both Abdul and my father are very proud men." She frowned and looked down at the ring she wore.

"You're frightened of how your father will accept our news?" He guessed at what was on her mind.

She smiled at him, as if pleased that he'd read her mind. "Frightened is too strong a word—concerned is more like it. Although I would have been far more concerned if I was going back to Tamir unmarried and pregnant." She sighed. "I just hate confrontation, and I know there is sure to be one with my father when we return."

A wave of protectiveness rose up inside him. "If and when you have that confrontation, you won't be having it alone. I'll be standing right next to you."

She flashed him a smile that once again sent a fluttering heat through him. He tightened his grip on the steering wheel and focused his attention on the road ahead.

Their conversation on the ride home remained light and easy. They talked about the landscape, the country of Montebello, and of the celebrations that would take place in five months' time when Prince Lucas would take the crown in January.

By the time they reached the outskirts of the piazza just outside the palace gates night was falling and they were both ready for another meal.

They returned the car to the rental place, then walked to the Red Dragon Inn for a late dinner. He could tell she was weary by the time they'd finished eating. As they walked back to the guest house, her eyes were drooping and she had grown quiet.

"I think the princess who used to love to stay up late has disappeared," he observed.

She stifled a yawn with the back of her hand, then laughed. "I don't know what's the matter with me lately. I can't seem to get enough sleep."

"That's because you're sleeping for two." He frowned as they entered the guest house. "Aren't you supposed to be taking special vitamins or something?"

"Yes, and as soon as we get back to Tamir I'll go to the doctor for the prescription and a complete check-up."

"That's important," Farid said. "My son must be strong and healthy."

She looked at him in surprise and he realized it was the first time he'd made reference to her baby being his. "And if it's a daughter?" she asked.

"Then she will be beautiful and healthy."

She patted the sofa next to her and he sat down. "What would you prefer, Farid? A son or a daughter?"

As always, when seated so close to her, his head was filled with her sweet feminine scent. When had he become so aware of her as a woman? Always before he'd managed to think of her as a princess...a sexless entity to be admired from afar, to be protected at all costs.

Funny, because he'd never had a long-term relationship with a woman, the possibility of having children had never entered his mind. Now he found himself contemplating the joys and heartaches of children.

"A boy will cause us sleepless nights. He'll fight our authority, ignore our curfews and take us to the brink of madness before he finally becomes a man." He smiled softly. "But, a girl...a girl will simply break our hearts."

"That is positively dismal," Samira exclaimed.

He laughed. "Ah, but amid the heartache will be the greatest joys of our lives. Boy or girl...as long as it's healthy, I'll love either."

She reached out and took one of his hands in hers. "Thank you, Farid. Simply saying thank you seems so inadequate for what you've done for me." Tears suddenly glistened in her eyes and she released his hand and stood. "I must be overtired, because I'm getting emotional. I think I'll just go on to bed."

"Good night, Samira."

She murmured a good-night, then disappeared into the bedroom. Farid remained seated on the sofa, thinking about the day's events.

Married. He was married to Princess Samira of

Tamir. He was responsible not only for her safety and for providing for her, but he was also responsible for her happiness. They had bound their lives together.

A temporary arrangement in all likelihood, he reminded himself.

She didn't love him and he didn't love her, but surely they could find some sense of contentment with one another for the time they shared together.

He admired many things about her. Her gentleness, her generosity and the quickness of her sweet smiles. She was more than easy to look at, and there had been moments over the past twenty-four hours when her smile and her touch had stoked a simmering ember of heat in the pit of his stomach.

"Farid?"

He turned toward the bedroom at the sound of her voice and his breath froze in his chest at the sight of her. She stood in the doorway, clad in a long, silky white nightgown with spaghetti straps. She looked lovelier than Farid had ever seen her before.

"If we are going to make my parents believe that we married for love, then it's important that we share the same bed." Her cheeks grew more and more pink as she spoke. "We should get accustomed to sharing a bed before we return to Tamir."

He nodded. "Then I'll be in there in just a few minutes."

"All right," she replied and once again disappeared from the doorway.

Farid drew in a deep breath. He hadn't thought about the sleeping arrangements. He hadn't considered that they would be sleeping side by side in the same bed.

When he had thought about marrying her, he hadn't considered the intimacy that was inherent in a marriage even if the two people involved weren't having sex.

Drawing another deep breath, he stood. It was no big deal, he told himself. He could sleep in the same bed with Samira.

He checked to make sure the doors were locked, then turned out the living-room light. Moonlight danced in the bedroom window, sending in enough illumination that he could easily see her on the right side of the bed, the sheet pulled up to just below her chin.

Her eyes were closed as if she'd already fallen asleep, but he knew she wasn't asleep by her irregular breathing. He knew by her pretending to be asleep she was hoping an awkward situation would be less awkward.

He moved to the empty side of the bed and eased down on the mattress. Quickly he removed his shoes and socks, then unstrapped the gun he'd been wearing on his ankle.

He normally wore the gun in a shoulder holster beneath his suit jacket, but since Samira had insisted he not wear his uniform the past two days, he now wore the gun hidden at his ankle.

He placed the loaded weapon on the nightstand, then pulled his shirt over his head and tossed it on a nearby chair. Samira's scent enveloped him, creating a small ball of heat in the pit of his stomach.

Why did he feel so ridiculously nervous? There had been times in his past working royal security that he had literally faced death, but he couldn't remember being as nervous as he was at this moment.

Standing up, he removed his slacks, then slid beneath the sheet. He lay on his back, afraid to move a single muscle as his mind filled with a vision of her in her nightgown.

The white of the gown had made her olive skin look rich and warm, and the upper portion of her breasts had been visible above the neckline.

The ball of heat in the pit of his stomach expanded as he thought how easy it would be to touch her skin right now. All he had to do was reach out across the width of the mattress, and he would encounter her warm, sweet skin.

He squeezed his eyes tightly closed in an attempt to banish the mental image and was instantly suffused with the memory of the brief kiss they had shared.

Despite the fact that his mouth had touched hers for only a moment, it had been long enough for him to recognize that her lips were achingly soft.

Farid sighed, realizing that he just might have underestimated the difficulty of the celibacy issue.

Chapter 6

Samira awoke as dawn's light was stealing through the window. Warmth. She was surrounded by it, a sweet warmth that made her reluctant to move.

She drifted in the twilight place between unconscious sleep and complete wakefulness, no conscious thoughts disturbing her overall sense of well-being and security.

It wasn't until she became aware of a strange noise that the last vestige of sleep fell away and complete consciousness swept in.

Farid.

Beneath her cheek she could feel his warm, firm flesh, and in an instant she realized she was lying sprawled across his bare chest and the sound that had awakened her was the faint snoring that emitted from him.

She had never awakened in a man's arms before and the pleasure she now felt caused her pulse to accelerate. His arm was around her, his hand resting in the small of her back with a sweet intimacy that sleep had bred.

She was afraid to move, and equally afraid not to. It would be embarrassing if he were to awaken and discover her shamelessly draped over him.

But she didn't want to leave the evocative warmth of his arms. She wanted to linger here, with his bare skin against hers, his male scent surrounding her. He smelled so wonderfully alien to her—a clean scent mixed with spicy cologne and a maleness that was intoxicating.

Cautiously, she raised her head, reassured when there was no break in his soft snoring. As he continued to sleep, she took the opportunity to study him.

His long, dark lashes cast spiderlike shadows beneath his eyes that gave him an air of vulnerability that was instantly appealing. His mouth was slightly open and his strong features appeared softer in sleep.

Last night had been the first time she'd ever heard him laugh, and she'd been stunned by how the wonderful sound had seemed to wrap itself around her heart.

In the past two days, since the moment he'd proposed to her, she'd seen a side of Farid she'd never seen before. There had been moments when he'd seemed softer...almost gentle. So unlike the arrogant, distant, unemotional man she'd believed him to be.

She found her gaze focused on his mouth and she

remembered the kiss they'd shared the day before at the end of their marriage ceremony.

The kiss had been brief…far too brief. But when his lips had touched hers, they had been sweetly warm and she now wondered what it would be like to receive a real, lingering kiss from him.

She closed her eyes and imagined it…his mouth taking possession of hers as his hands tangled in her hair. His tongue seeking hers as he sought to deepen the kiss. Ah, the vision took her breath away.

She opened her eyes and squeaked in surprise as she realized he was awake and gazing at her. She quickly rolled over onto her own side of the bed, aware of a small grin of amusement curving his lips.

"Good morning," he said.

"Good morning," she murmured as she closed her eyes and fought off a sudden wave of nausea. Apparently she'd moved too quickly. Morning sickness threatened to overtake her.

"Are you all right?" His voice held a residual bit of sleepiness in it, making it deeper than usual and oddly provocative.

She didn't open her eyes, in truth was afraid to. She wasn't sure she was ready to see him all tousle-haired and bare-chested. "I'm okay. I'm just feeling a little bit nauseous."

"Then just lay here and relax," he said. "It's still early."

She felt him get out of bed. She heard the rustling noise of clothing and knew he was getting dressed. She kept her eyes closed and some of her tension left her as she heard the sound of the bathrooom door opening, then closing.

She wasn't sure which was worse, the awkwardness of waking up in a bed with a man she hardly knew, or the queasiness that threatened to erupt into something worse at any moment.

At least the morning sickness had alleviated some of the embarrassment of waking up to find herself draped over Farid like a blanket.

She heard the bathroom door open once again and gasped in surprise as a cool compress was laid across her forehead. Her eyes sprang open. Farid stood by the side of the bed, gazing down at her with undisguised concern.

"Thank you," she said as she reached up to touch the cool, folded cloth.

He nodded. "I don't know if it will help or not, but it's the only thing I knew to do."

"It's helping already," she replied. She forced a smile. "Don't look so worried. Morning sickness is perfectly normal."

"Does it last long?"

"I hope not," she said. "Actually, I've heard it usually passes within the third or fourth month of pregnancy."

His look of concern eased somewhat. "Is there anything else I can do for you? Anything I can get for you?"

"No, thanks. I'll just lie here a few more minutes and it will pass."

He shifted from one foot to the other as if reluctant to go, yet eager to leave. "Then I'll just let you rest."

She watched as he left the room and pulled the bedroom door closed behind him. Her thoughts were filled with him.

Farid Nasir.

Her husband.

She looked at the slender band of gold that encircled her finger. The ring was simple and relatively inexpensive, but the thought that it had been his mother's and he'd given it to Samira, touched her. As did the fact that he had made her a cold compress for her head.

She reached up and turned the cloth over. Farid Nasir was a man of many facets. She'd believed him to be cold and arrogant, and there was a touch of those qualities in him, but there were so many others to explore as well.

She knew now that he had a wonderful sense of humor. She'd not only seen it sparkling from his eyes, but had heard it in the robust laughter he'd released the night before.

He also had a surprisingly gentle center, displayed as he'd held the lost little girl in the piazza, exhibited when he'd spoken of the baby she carried and apparent in the gift of a cold compress for her head.

A tiny alarm went off in the back of her mind. Take care, Samira, she told herself. The last thing she would want to do was to make herself believe that she was falling in love with Farid.

He was a man who had made it clear in a dozen

different ways that he didn't believe in the romantic kind of love she'd always dreamed about, a man who had made it more than clear that he had married her for duty and duty only.

She smiled at herself and her own foolishness. She wasn't falling in love with Farid, she was just feeling overly grateful for the compress on her head and that he'd agreed to love the child she carried despite the fact that the baby wasn't his.

A mental picture of Desmond filled her mind and brought with it a surprising lack of emotion. There was no love, nor was there any hatred. There was simply a vague distaste when she thought of the man she had believed she'd loved.

She sighed softly as Desmond's image was usurped by one of Farid. Desmond might be handsome, but so was Farid. And while Desmond might be wonderfully charming, he lacked the qualities that Farid possessed...qualities like integrity and honor.

And it had been honor and duty that had driven Farid to marry her, she had to remember that. No matter how pleasant she found his laughter, no matter how wonderful it was to awaken in his arms, he'd married her for one reason and one reason alone—duty. And she absolutely, positively had to remember that.

She'd made a stupid mistake in sleeping with Desmond Caruso, but she had a feeling it would be a far bigger mistake to fall in love with Farid.

She awakened some time later, surprised that she had apparently drifted back to sleep. The sun pouring through the windows let her know it was midmorning, and her first thought was of her husband.

Her husband. Farid. What had he been doing in the hours that she'd slept? What did he do in his hours of leisure, when he wasn't in charge of her safety? Did he have hobbies? Did he like to read or watch television? Did he enjoy crossword puzzles or other challenging mind games?

After she'd showered and dressed for the day, she left the bedroom to find him sitting on the sofa and thumbing through a newspaper.

"Good morning again," he said and closed the newspaper.

"'Morning." She gestured toward the paper. "Anything interesting?"

"Same old stuff. How are you feeling?"

"Much better, thank you."

He stood and held out a small envelope. "This was delivered for you while you were sleeping."

"What is it?" she asked.

"I don't know. I didn't open it. It's addressed to you."

She took it from him and opened it. "It's from Queen Gwendolyn…an invitation to dinner this evening." She laid the envelope on the coffee table. "I'll send my regrets."

"Why?" Farid looked at her curiously.

"I don't know…" She stared down at the gold band around her finger. "I'm not ready to return to Tamir yet, but if I introduce you to Queen Gwendolyn and King Marcus as my husband, then I'm certain word will get back to my father immediately.''

"Then you go as Princess Samira and I go as your bodyguard," he said. "We pretend nothing has changed and you have dinner with the king and queen."

She looked back up at him. "But that doesn't seem right."

He smiled, causing the tiny lines at the outer edges of his eyes to deepen. "I appreciate the sentiment, but it would not do to turn down the queen and king's invitation. For the first time in years, Montebello and Tamir are enjoying good relations. You would not want to offend the king and queen. Besides, we'll have plenty of time to attend social gatherings and such as husband and wife when you decide it's time to return to Tamir."

She looked at him gratefully. He was making things so easy on her. Another man might balk at being relegated to the role of bodyguard when he was married to a princess.

It wasn't until later that evening, when they were walking from the guest house to the palace that she remembered to ask him about his hobbies.

"What do you do in your spare time, Farid?" The evening air was laden with scents, but none as familiar and comforting as the scent that emanated from Farid.

Amazing that in less than two days she'd learned the masculine smell of him, the spicy cologne coupled with clean maleness.

"Being a bodyguard to a princess leaves very little spare time," he replied. "But when I do have time there are several things I enjoy."

"Like what?" she asked. He looked so handsome in his uniform, and she felt a slight quiver in her stomach as she thought that once again tonight they would be sleeping beneath the same sheet, in the same bed.

"All of the men who serve as bodyguards work out a lot and we're a competitive bunch. We have frequent physical challenges. I also enjoy target practice, and I like to run long-distance."

Samira was instantly granted a mental image of Farid clad only in a pair of jogging shorts, his body covered with a sheen of perspiration as he ran. The image was so evocative, so powerful, she stumbled and would have fallen had Farid not caught her by the arm to steady her.

His touch sent her pulse rate skittering to a new frantic pace and she quickly stepped away from his grip. "Thanks, I'm fine," she murmured.

"You're trembling," he said, his dark eyes watching her closely. "Are you nervous about the dinner?"

Samira grasped at his suggestion. "Yes, a little." In truth, she hadn't been nervous until this very moment. "I was just thinking...what if Desmond is at dinner? I'm not sure if I'm ready to see him so soon."

Farid stopped walking and stood before her. He gently placed his hands on her shoulders, his dark eyes unreadable in the shadows of the falling night. "He only has the power over you that you give him."

"He has no power over me," she exclaimed. She averted her gaze from Farid. "It would just be awkward, that's all."

What was really awkward was speaking to the man she had married about the man she'd made love with three months before.

They fell silent as they reached the palace and Farid fell back several steps to his place as bodyguard. The moment they entered the palace, Farid disappeared as Samira was led into a large solarium at the back of the palace.

The solarium was beautiful, decorated in creams and golds and with a breathtaking view of the lush gardens and beyond that the blue of the ocean. As she entered, Prince Lucas rose from one of the elegant sofas and greeted her.

"Princess Samira." The handsome, dark-haired prince took her hand in his. "It's nice to see you again. It has been far too long."

"Prince Lucas, it's wonderful to see you back here in Montebello where you belong," she replied.

"It's good to be back home." Although he said the words, there seemed to be shadowed sadness in his eyes that belied them.

"You look well," she said.

"Thank you, and you're as pretty as ever. Your family is well?"

"They are very well," she replied.

At that moment Queen Gwendolyn and King Marcus joined them. King Marcus was a handsome man with thick white hair and dark eyes. Queen Gwendoyln's beauty was legendary. A blue-eyed blonde with delicate, aristocratic features, she was known not only for her beauty, but for her warmth as well.

That warmth was apparent as she greeted Samira. "We'll wait just a moment for Lorenzo and Eliza to join us," she said. The four of them chatted for a few minutes before Lorenzo and Eliza appeared and they all went into the adjoining dining room.

Like the solarium, the dining room was decorated in creams and golds with deep-green accents.

Samira breathed a sigh of relief as she realized it was only going to be the six of them for dinner. At least she wouldn't have to sit across from Desmond Caruso and make nice to the man.

Dinner was sumptuous, but throughout the meal, Samira couldn't help but notice the profound changes that seemed to have taken place in Prince Lucas.

Over the years, before his disappearance and his bout with amnesia, she had attended functions with him and had always found him to be a natural charmer with a wonderful sense of humor and a touch of irreverence. His blue eyes had always sparkled, and he'd had a reputation for being something of a ladies' man.

There was no hint of that man now. He seemed more somber and again Samira sensed a deep sadness inside him. Or perhaps it was maturity, she told herself. After all, in less than six months time he would be taking on more responsibility and preparing to eventually take the crown as King.

Lorenzo, King Sebestiani's godson and nephew, on

the other hand, looked wonderfully happy and it was obvious he and his wife, Eliza, were madly in love.

Throughout the meal, Samira thought again and again of Farid, wondering if he was eating a meal as good as hers, if he was being entertained by friendly people. She'd not worn the gold wedding ring and she was surprised that her finger felt naked without it.

Almost as soon as the meal was over, King Marcus, Lorenzo and Prince Lucas excused themselves, leaving Queen Gwendolyn, Eliza and Samira to enjoy their after-dinner coffee alone.

The two women spoke of their families and of the charity work they were each involved in.

"I have not spoken with Rashid and Julia for the past week," Queen Gwendolyn said. "I understand they are enjoying some time on Erimos."

Samira nodded. Erimos was an isolated island where her brother, Rashid, enjoyed spending time with his wife, Julia Sebastiani Kamal, and their son, Omar. "Little Omar is growing like a weed."

"He is the light of our lives." Queen Gwendolyn smiled at Eliza. "King Marcus and I are hoping to be blessed with many grandchildren."

"It must be wonderful to have Prince Lucas back," Samira said, changing the subject.

"Yes, it is wonderful to have him home. I can't tell you of my pain when I thought he might be gone forever." Her blue eyes darkened slightly. "There's nothing worse than losing a child."

"He seems different somehow...more pensive."

Samira hoped she hadn't overstepped herself in broaching the subject.

A small frown tugged at Queen Gwendoyln's lovely features and she stared down into her coffee cup for a long moment before she looked at Samira once again.

"My son is suffering an enormous heartbreak," she said softly, her pain for her son evident in her voice, in the shadows of her eyes.

"A heartbreak?" Samira had heard no gossip linking the handsome prince to any woman.

Queen Gwendolyn sighed. "It seems he became quite close to a woman in Colorado while he was there, and only recently he discovered she has died."

"Oh, I'm so sorry," Samira exclaimed.

The queen smiled, a sad little smile. "If he fell and hurt his knee, I could put a bandage on it and make it all better. If he was fevered, I could cool his forehead with a damp cloth. But, I fear when it comes to matters of the heart and the pain of loss, a mother is helpless to make that pain go away."

Samira wasn't sure how to reply. Her heart ached for the handsome prince whose eyes radiated such sadness. As she thought of the baby she carried, she felt an affinity with the queen, a mother who would do anything in her power to ease the pain of a son.

They visited for another hour, then Samira and the queen parted and Farid rejoined Samira for the walk back to their guest house.

"You had a nice time?" Farid asked as they walked.

"I did. The king and queen are warm, gracious people. Prince Lucas joined us. Did you know he worked undercover for the FBI and infiltrated the Brothers of Darkness?" The Brothers of Darkness was a terrorist group that had been wreaking havoc both in Montebello and Tamir.

"I'd heard rumors."

"He spoke a little bit about it at dinner," she explained.

"The Brothers of Darkness brought a lot of misery to the people in both countries by their indiscriminate bombings of public places. They were suspected of bombing the airport here a month ago, but I believe the villain turned out to be an airport security person."

She nodded as they entered the garden that would eventually lead them to their guest house. They had spoken of it at dinner.

They had gone only a few steps when Samira spied a male figure coming down the narrow sidewalk toward them.

He was Desmond's height and approximate weight. Panic swept through her. She wasn't ready to see him yet. She didn't want any kind of a confrontation with him.

Frantically, she looked for a place to hide and seeing nowhere to go, she impulsively wrapped her arms around Farid's neck and pulled his head down so she could meet his lips with hers. Her ploy was to use him to shield her from whomever it was who approached.

Farid gave a gasp of surprise, but his mouth complied with her wishes as his arms encircled her and pulled her close. So close…too wonderfully close. Her body was intimately pressed against his as her fingers encountered the soft, thick hair at the nape of his neck.

Somewhere in the back of her mind, she had known instinctively that Farid would be good at kissing, but nothing had prepared her for the flames of heat that shot through her as his lips plied hers.

Instantly any thoughts of Desmond and the reasons why she'd instigated the kiss in the first place were gone, banished by the sweet sensations that swept through her as the kiss lingered.

Tentatively, his tongue sought to deepen the kiss and she welcomed him, her tongue swirling with his. Vaguely, she was aware of footsteps passing them by and growing softer until they disappeared altogether.

Her heartbeat banged against her ribs…or was it his heartbeat she felt racing so frantically as his hands moved up and down her back in firm, caressing strokes?

It was he who broke the kiss. "Samira," he said as he tore his mouth from hers. "What do you think you're doing?" His voice held an edge of anger as he took two steps back from her.

"I'm…sorry." The heat of embarrassment swept up her neck and warmed her cheeks. "I just…I thought…"

"I know exactly why you kissed me," he interrupted her, his eyes blazing with unsuppressed anger.

"I know we have a deal where this marriage is concerned, that it is to be a marriage in name only. But, I'll tell you this, Samira, the next time you kiss me like that, all bets are off. I will not be responsible for my actions."

Chapter 7

Farid felt as if he'd swallowed a time bomb and was waiting for the inevitable explosion to follow. He and Samira had been married for a full week. He'd not only spent each moment of every day with her, but each torturous minute of each night as well.

They were now lying side by side on one of the white sand beaches Montebello had to offer. Samira had awakened just before noon and announced that she wanted to spend the day at the beach. "I won't be able to wear a regular bathing suit for too much longer," she'd said.

The sun was hot overhead, but not hot enough to burn the tension out of Farid. It was a tension that had been building for the past seven days.

He would have been fine had they not shared that kiss a week before. That damnable kiss in the garden had awakened a hunger in him that he couldn't seem to banish.

The moment she'd thrown her arms around his neck, he'd known what had prompted her actions. He'd seen the man approaching them, a man who in the darkness had the build and height of Desmond Caruso, and he'd known the kiss had been an effort on her part to hide her face. But that hadn't stopped him from responding to it.

Even now, thinking of the honey sweetness of her mouth caused a heat to boil up inside him that had nothing to do with the sun overhead.

Making matters worse was the fact that she was lying next to him in a bright yellow two-piece bathing suit that merely served to increase his internal temperature.

He sat up and tried to stare out at the ocean, knowing he needed to focus on the sensation of cool waves breaking over his heated body. But his gaze was continually drawn to Samira.

She lay on her back, her eyes closed, and he suspected from the deep rhythm of her breathing that she'd fallen asleep.

The blanket beneath them was a mint green that enhanced the darkness of her hair and the rich tones of her skin. The bathing suit, while certainly more modest than a bikini, exposed far too much to his gaze.

The upper curve of her breasts was visible above the top, looking achingly touchable. The bottoms hugged her hips and were cut high on her thighs, exposing an indecent length of shapely legs.

Her lower abdomen had the beginnings of a small pouch, the visual proof of the baby that was growing inside her. Farid fought the impulse to reach over and place his palm against the smooth skin. He knew to indulge himself in such an intimate touch would in all likelihood detonate the bomb inside him.

What made it even worse was that he knew she was aware of the sexual tension between them. There were moments when her eyes glowed with the knowledge of it, when he could swear she was thinking the same thoughts that he was…what would it be like if they made love?

Would they be good together? Would their bodies fit and would they instinctively know how to please one another? Every second of every day these thoughts filled Farid's head.

He frowned, wishing he could run to the ocean edge and dive into the waves. An energetic swim would do much to ease the tension inside him. But there was no way he'd leave Samira's side, not even to take a quick dip in the ocean.

Not only did he have the problem of the internal stress of Samira's near-nakedness so close to him, there was also the issue of the blond-haired man who was becoming far too familiar a sight.

He scanned the beach area now, both unsurprised and unsettled to see the man seated on a bench a short distance from them. The man seemed to be paying them no attention whatsoever. A newspaper was opened on the bench next to him and he seemed simply to be enjoying reading the news in the brightness of the sun.

Farid returned his attention to Samira as he heard her stir. She sat up and shot him a quick smile. "Sorry, I didn't mean to drift off to sleep."

"That's all right. You must have needed it."

"It seems like that's all I do, sleep and eat." She smiled at him.

"That's not true. You've lunched with the queen and sat in the royal box at a polo match."

She nodded. "Queen Gwendolyn and King Marcus have been very hospitable. Why don't you go swimming? You've been just sitting here for the last hour. You must be hot and I'm sure a dip would be refreshing."

"I'm fine. Besides, I wouldn't be comfortable leaving you here by yourself to go swimming," he replied.

"Farid, I appreciate your conscientiousness to your duty, but I'm sure I'll be just fine right here on this blanket if you want to take a swim."

"Well, I'm not so sure," he replied.

She looked at him sharply. "Why? What's wrong?"

He hesitated a moment before answering. He certainly didn't want to give her any unwarranted worry, but he also didn't want her completely in the dark should a threat rise up.

"See that man over there? The one on the bench

reading the paper?'' He inclined his head in the direction of the man.

Her gaze shot in that direction, then she looked back at Farid. "Yes…what about him?''

"He was in the restaurant where we had dinner last night and also when we had lunch this afternoon. Now he's here.''

Samira shot another glance over to the man, a frown creating a wrinkle across the width of her forehead. "Do you think he's following us?''

"I don't know,'' Farid replied. "I suppose it's possible that it's just a coincidence that he's shown up in the places we've been for the past two days.''

"You don't sound convinced of that.''

He shrugged. "I take nothing for granted and I prefer to rely on my instincts more than anything else.''

She pulled her knees up to her chest, her gaze not wavering from him. "And what do your instincts tell you in this case?''

He shot a quick glance back at the man, who still seemed completely absorbed in his reading. "I'm not sure,'' he confessed. He looked back at her. "I just think we need to be extra careful. We both know the risks that come with your position and now we have not only your safety to worry about, but that of your child as well.''

He was sorry for speaking his thoughts aloud when he saw the frown that once again marred her lovely face. "I shouldn't have told you this,'' he said, cursing his own stupidity. "I didn't mean to upset you.''

She reached out and placed her hand on his forearm. "No, I'm glad you did." She quickly withdrew her hand from him. "I need to know if there might be a problem."

She'd been very careful over the past week, since the night of their kiss and his words of warning, not to touch him in any way. They gave each other a wide berth in the cottage and tried not to invade each other's personal space.

Except in the early mornings, when inevitably their bodies sought one another in sleep. Every morning he awakened with her in his arms and pretended to sleep until she'd awakened and quickly moved away.

He enjoyed those moments of holding her far too much, had come to anticipate the morning when her body would seek the warmth of his and in the unselfconsciousness of sleep she cuddled close to him.

She sighed and raced a hand through her shoulder-length hair, then stared out at the ocean waves in the distance. "This past week has been rather idyllic, hasn't it?"

He knew she was thinking of the hours they had spent driving to small towns and sightseeing. Each day they had chosen a new place to visit. Their conversations had been pleasant, their silences companionable.

Farid would have characterized the last week as idyllic also, had it not been for the hunger that had been awakened in him for her with the kiss they had shared.

"Yes, it has," he agreed.

"Kind of like a break from reality," she added.

"It's been nice to be someplace where nobody recognizes me."

Farid said nothing, but once again shot a glance at the blond-haired man. He hoped she was right. He hoped she hadn't been recognized and the man's presence was merely a silly coincidence.

"I think perhaps I've had enough sun for one day," she said as she reached for her bathing-suit cover-up. "What about you?"

"I'm ready to go if you are." He stood and held a hand out to help her up. She allowed him to help her stand, then instantly removed her hand from his.

They were both being so very careful, he thought as they packed up their items and headed back to the rental car. No lingering touches, no physical contact that wasn't absolutely warranted.

How long could they continue avoiding each other's touch? How long could they be satisfied with only those moments in the early dawn when they came together as if their skin hungered for touch?

Eventually Farid knew something was going to break…he just wasn't sure what kind of a break it would be. One thing was clear—the tension between them couldn't continue to build without something happening.

He wondered if she felt the same kind of sexual frustration that he did. Surely she felt the energy between them that sparked with electricity?

Not that it mattered. He would never break the condition of their marriage that forbade him making love to her. He would never break the condition…unless she asked him to.

And there were moments in the night, when he was lying next to her, listening to the sound of her soft breathing, smelling the feminine scent of her and feeling her body warmth, that he desperately wished she would ask him.

It would probably be better, though, if they did not break that particular condition. With each day that passed Farid was more and more convinced that their marriage would probably only last until they reached the shores of Tamir.

She had spoken the truth when she had said their time in Montebello had been a break from reality. When she returned to the bosom of her family, he had little doubt that this marriage would end.

She was quiet on the ride back to the palace grounds and again he kicked himself for speaking his apprehensions about the blond-haired man aloud. He hadn't intended to worry her, but apparently he had.

When they were back in the guest house, he went into his smaller bedroom where his clothes were and quickly changed into a clean pair of shorts and a shirt. He assumed she had gone into the master suite to change as well. But when he returned to the living room he found her standing at the window staring out, still clad in her bright yellow swimsuit cover-up.

He cursed himself for causing her undue concern and reminding her of one of the negative aspects of her position. As a princess of Tamir, she had been raised knowing that kidnapping attempts, even death threats, would be a part of her life.

"You know, Samira, it's possible that man hasn't been following us for any bad reason. Perhaps he's merely smitten with your beauty."

She whirled around from the window to look at him. "Be serious," she exclaimed with a scornful look.

"What makes you think I'm not being serious?" he asked.

She moved away from the window. "Nadia and Leila are the true beauties of the family," she said, referring to her two sisters. "I'm the plain one of the bunch."

He looked at her in surprise. "Surely you don't really believe that?" But he could tell by the look in her eyes that she did believe it and it stunned him.

"Samira," he said softly. Although someplace in the back of his mind, he knew it was dangerous to touch her, he placed his hands on her slender shoulders, forcing her to look at him as he spoke to her.

"You're right, both Nadia and Leila are beautiful women. Their beauty is like the sunshine…bright and intense. They have the kind of beauty that shouts at you, but you…" He couldn't help himself. He reached up and stroked a strand of her shining dark hair.

He wondered what in the hell he thought he was doing, yet was unable to stop himself from the sheer pleasure of touching her.

His fingers left her hair and he caressed down the

silky skin of her cheek. "Your beauty is like the moonlight," he began. The sudden light that shone from her lovely almond-shaped eyes heated his insides. "Your beauty is soft and subtle and it whispers like a gentle breeze."

He suddenly felt embarrassed by his uncharacteristic poetic feelings, and he dropped his hand from her cheek and stepped back.

But she refused to allow him any distance. She moved to stand directly before him once again, their bodies only a breath away from each other.

She reached up and placed her palm on his cheek and in that instant a powerful desire for her welled up inside him. Her eyes were deep waters and he felt himself on the verge of drowning in them.

"That was the most beautiful thing anyone has ever said to me," she said, so close to him her breath was warm on his face.

"I meant every word," he replied, wondering if she could hear the fierce pounding of his heartbeat, or feel the rigid tension that suffused his body. With the simple touch of her hand to his face, she'd unleashed the desire that Farid had been fighting against for the past week.

"Farid, if you don't kiss me right now, I think I might die." Her voice was a soft plea and her lower lip trembled with emotion.

He felt them teetering on the edge of a precipice, knew that if he kissed her it was possible they would plunge off the cliff and into an uncharted and perhaps disturbing alien territory.

"I told you before, Samira, if I kiss you, I can't be responsible for any consequences that may follow."

"I promise you I don't intend to hold you responsible," she replied.

The words, coupled with the longing in her eyes, shoved aside the last of any reservations Farid might have entertained.

He claimed her mouth with his and wrapped her in his arms, pulling her tightly against him. Her lips met his eagerly as she pressed intimately against him, her body soft and warm.

She tasted just as he remembered…hot and sweet, and he used his tongue to deepen the kiss, swirling it with hers as the fever inside him grew to mammoth proportions.

He ran his hands up and down her back and knew they were close enough that she would know the full extent of his desire for her.

He broke the kiss, aware that both of them were breathless, but instead of releasing her, he moved his lips to the hollow of her throat.

Her skin tasted of sunshine and the salty ocean air and Farid knew he'd never tasted anything more intoxicating.

She dropped her head back with a low moan as her fingers tangled in his hair. "Make love to me, Farid, she whispered. "Please, take me into our bedroom and make love to me."

With an effort, he dropped his arms from around her and stepped back. Her eyes glowed with an inner fever and her lips were slightly swollen from his kiss.

He wanted her. He'd never felt such desire for a woman, but he didn't want the heat of the moment to cause her to make a decision she would later regret.

"Are you sure that's what you want?" he asked.

"I'm sure." Her eyes clouded with doubt. "But...if you don't want me..."

How could she doubt his desire for her? Couldn't she feel it raging from him? Hadn't she tasted his hunger in his kiss? The fact that she was so unsure of his wanting her touched him deeply, and once again he drew her into his embrace.

"I want you, Samira. I've been half-mad with wanting you since that night we kissed in the gardens," he said. "Lying in bed next to you night after night and not touching you has driven me insane. I can't think of anything else but my wanting of you."

"Then take me to our bed and show me."

He didn't wait for her to ask again. He swept her up into his arms and carried her to the master suite. As he laid her on the bed, he had a single disturbing thought. When he made love to her and she closed her eyes, would she be thinking of him...her husband?

Or would she be fantasizing that she was making love to another man—the man who was the father of her baby—Desmond Caruso?

As Farid joined her on the bed and once again claimed her mouth with his, Samira felt herself falling into a maelstrom of sensations and emotions she'd never before experienced.

He had seduced her with his sweet words, but it was a seduction she'd welcomed—even encouraged. But it wasn't just his words that had seduced her. It was also the intimacy of their living arrangements for the past week, the quiet strength that radiated from him day and night, the gentle caring he exhibited when she was tired or suffering a bout of morning sickness.

He'd seduced her by being the kind of man he was...a man of honor and dignity, a man who was so much more than she'd once believed him to be.

His mouth plied hers with heat, a flame she welcomed in response. She'd hungered for him ever since that night in the garden when they'd shared their first real kiss. The memory of the taste of his lips, the feel of his arms around her, had played and replayed in her mind in the week that had passed.

As the kiss continued, she moved her hands to the buttons of his shirt, wanting to feel his broad, firm chest and warm skin beneath her fingertips.

Lying in the same bed with him night after night, feeling the heat that radiated from his body, knowing he wore nothing but boxer shorts, had evoked a hunger in her...a hunger to touch his warm skin, a hunger to have him touch her.

As she fumbled with the buttons of his shirt, he worked the buttons that ran down the front of her bathing-suit cover-up. He tore his lips from hers and shrugged out of his shirt, then raised her up to help her rid herself of the gauzy material that covered her.

Instantly she was gifted with his smooth, firm chest

making contact with her breasts, the only barrier between them her thin bathing-suit top.

Again their mouths met, this time in frenzied need. She ran her hands over the width of his back, reveling in the feel of solid muscles beneath the warm skin.

She gasped as his hands splayed to cover her breasts. Even through the fabric, his touch was intensely pleasurable. His lips left hers and trailed a path down her neck, shooting electric currents through her at every point of contact.

His hands left her breasts and caressed down her sides and across her lower abdomen, then swept down to lightly stroke the inside of her thighs.

He seemed to be in no hurry. His caresses became slow and languid, as if he were savoring each and every inch of her skin.

It was only by the intense glow in his eyes and the uneven rhythm of his breathing that she knew he was as lost in waves of desire as she was.

By the time he reached behind her to unfasten her bathing-suit top, she was ready for their intimacy to deepen, and as his hands covered her bare breasts, a moan escaped her.

"Samira." He said her name softly, almost reverently as his thumbs razed over the throbbing tips of her breasts. "You are so beautiful."

Beneath his touch and in his gaze she felt her own beauty for the first time in her life. It resonated inside her, a new and wonderful feeling.

He made her feel not only beautiful, but desirable

as well, and she wanted to give back to him the feelings he stirred in her.

But before she could tell him how beautiful she found him, before she could put into words how handsome he was, how he moved her, his mouth captured the tip of her breast and the ability to speak was lost in the vortex of sensation that engulfed her.

He teased her nipples, licking and nibbling the turgid tips until she thought she'd go mad, and when she thought she could stand no more, he eased her swimming-suit bottoms off her and touched her where she needed his touch most.

Tenderly, yet with mastery, he took her higher and higher. It frightened her just a little, the incredible tension that built inside her. But her fear was overwhelmed by the explosion of sensations that swept through her, leaving her shattered and gasping and weak in his arms.

Only then did he kick off his shorts and briefs and take full and total possession of her.

She'd thought herself completely sated, but as he eased into her, a new hunger awakened in her. He released a moan of such pleasure it echoed in her veins and stirred her to heights she'd never known existed.

As he stroked slowly, deeply into her, her heart threatened to beat right out of her chest and she feared she might die from the exquisite, intense pleasure.

Agai he seemed to be in no hurry. With a languid rhythm he moved against her…into her, building inside her a conflagration that threatened to consume her.

She cried out, she thought she might have said his name, but she wasn't certain. Her cry seemed to snap whatever control he'd retained. With a guttural moan that came from the very depths of him, he increased his rhythm.

Faster and faster they moved together, hips locked, hands gripping and breaths gasping until she was once again tumbling over the edge and this time she took him with her. He stiffened against her as wave after wave of sensation swept through her.

Afterward, he rolled off and to her side, his arm around her as if he were reluctant to break all physical contact with her. Neither of them spoke for long moments.

"Are you all right?" he finally asked as he reached up and softly stroked her hair.

She snuggled closer against his side, loving the way their bodies fit together. "I'm fine. More than fine, actually."

"I didn't hurt you?"

"Of course not," she assured him.

They fell into a silence again. She was grateful he didn't move to get up, to leave her. She liked lying in his arms, feeling his hand smoothing over her hair, his body against hers.

There were so many things Samira wanted to say…to ask. She wondered if making love to him would always be as wonderful as it had just been. She wanted to tell him how amazing it had been.

Had it been as wonderful for him? She wished he'd tell her. She wished she could ask him. But, she feared that if she asked him, he would tell her that he was simply doing his duty. Nothing more, nothing less.

Chapter 8

Homesick.

Farid had never believed he could feel homesick
for his country, but after two and a half weeks in
Montebello, that's exactly how he felt. And he knew
Samira felt it, too.

It was another gorgeous day in Montebello, the sun
bright overhead in a cloudless blue sky. He and
Samira sat at a small round patio table, sipping cold
citrus drinks.

The restaurant served only sandwiches and drinks
and had very little seating inside, but had a dozen
umbrella tables in front of the establishment.

Around them, as usual, the piazza teamed with people and noise, and for the past half an hour the two
of them had been people-watching.

He knew Samira was homesick because in the past

few days she'd spoken longingly of home, but hadn't mentioned being ready to return.

He wasn't sure what she was waiting for, but knew she couldn't put off the inevitable forever. Eventually they would have to return to Tamir and together they would have to face her parents.

Farid couldn't guess what Sheik Ahmed's reaction might be to the news of their marriage and Samira's pregnancy. Certainly the sheik's temper was legendary and Farid had a feeling he certainly wouldn't be thrilled with their news.

In the back of his head, Farid still believed Samira would crumble and want out of the marriage once they returned to Tamir.

She would buckle beneath her father's questions and would end up telling him the truth. Once that happened, there was no way to guess what the future would bring.

He gazed at Samira now, wondering if she had any idea of how lovely she looked. Clad in a dark-pink dress that complemented her dark eyes and hair, she looked warm and alive and achingly touchable.

He took a sip of his cold drink in an attempt to cool the eternal flame that had ignited in him since the night they'd made love a week before.

"I've been thinking about names," she said as she stirred her drink with the straw. "Do you have any preferences?"

"I'm pretty partial to mine. I don't see any reason to choose a new one," he replied teasingly.

He was rewarded by her laughter and she gave him

a playful slap on the arm. "I'm being serious, Farid," she exclaimed, her dark eyes sparkling prettily. She set her glass down. "What was your mother's name?"

"It doesn't matter," he replied, the familiar tightness pressing against his ribs as thoughts of his mother fluttered through his mind. Would the anger never cease? "I think it better to give children their own names rather than name them for somebody."

He realized his voice had held a harsh edge and she looked at him in surprise. "I'd still like to know the name of the woman whose ring I wear," she said.

Farid sighed, realizing it was easier to tell her than to make a big deal out of not telling her. "Raisa. Her name was Raisa."

"Raisa." She looked down at the ring on her finger, then back to him. "That's a beautiful name. And your father's?"

"Hashim." This one came more easily to his lips and brought with it not only the warmth of love, but also the ache of enormous loss.

She picked up her glass again and took a sip, her gaze never leaving his face. "Why are you so angry with your mother?"

"I'm not," he replied, guessing that the words sounded as false to her as they did to his own ears. "I just don't want to name my daughter after her." He knew his answer hadn't satisfied her. "Let it go, Samira," he said softly. "It's a complicated issue."

She studied him another long moment, then he saw the corners of her lips curve upward in a faint smile.

"Okay, then if we have a boy we'll call him Bubba, and if it's a girl we'll call her LulaBelle."

He knew she was trying to get a rise out of him and he returned her grin, shoving aside thoughts of his mother. "How did you know those are my favorite names of all time?" he said, refusing to rise to her baiting.

Again he was granted the luxury of her laughter. For a moment, he tried to imagine his life without the sound of her laughter and was struck with a feeling of bereavement that twisted his insides.

She turned her attention to the people passing by the restaurant patio area and he kept his attention focused on her.

Making love with her had been a big mistake. In his wildest dreams he hadn't imagined that making love to Samira would be so wonderful.

She had been far more responsive, far more passionate and giving than he'd ever dreamed possible. He'd been intoxicated by the taste of her, the feminine scent of her. He'd been exhilarated by her sweet sighs and her throaty moans as he'd taken complete and total possession of her.

"You're staring at me, Farid," Samira now said, her cheeks coloring a becoming shade of pink as she directed her gaze back at him.

"It's one of the pleasures of being your husband," he replied. "Didn't you know that in our marriage contract it says I have the right to stare at you?"

She gifted him with a teasing smile. "Does that mean as your wife I have the right to stare at you, too?"

"Of course," he said. "Marriage is an equal opportunity staring institution."

She leaned across the table, her chin cupped in her hand and stared at him unabashedly, the teasing smile still curving the corners of her luscious lips.

It bothered him, how much he liked her smiles, how much he loved those early morning minutes when he awakened to find her, warm and sleeping in his arms.

It bothered him that he enjoyed her laughter, that he found so many of her habits endearing rather than irritating. In the past two weeks of their marriage, he'd become far too taken with her presence in his life, and he knew that was dangerous.

The worst thing he could do was to convince himself that anything about their arrangement was permanent. She'd married him on the rebound, frantic with worry and heartbroken by another man.

She was a woman who believed in and had dreamed of a romantic valentines-and-flowers kind of love that he would never be able to give her.

She had married him for expediency, not for love. She had slept with him because they were husband and wife. She had slept with Desmond Caruso because she believed herself in love with him.

Over the past week he'd fought with himself to keep from making love to her again, knowing that it would only make it more difficult for them both when they returned to Tamir and she left him. Nor had she made any move toward making love, as if she, too, knew it would only make the inevitable more painful.

He took another sip of his drink, returning her steady gaze. "Surely you can't find that much interesting to look at in this face," he said dryly.

"On the contrary, I find your features very fascinating." To his surprise she reached out and placed her palm on his cheek, her fingers cool from the glass they'd been holding.

It was the first time she'd consciously touched him since the night they had made love and it electrified him with immediate want.

"Your features are filled with such strength," she said softly. Her fingers warmed as they lingered on his skin. "You radiate determination and authority, and a confidence that is not only admirable, but appealing."

Again her cheeks reddened slightly, but she didn't remove her hand from him. Instead she trailed her fingertips down his cheek, across the line of his jaw, then lightly brushed them across his mouth.

It was the most seductive, provocative thing she'd ever done and he grabbed her fingers and kissed them. "If you continue to look at me that way, to touch me, then we'll be in bed before the day is over and I'm not talking about sleeping."

She laughed, a deep, throaty laugh that he'd never heard before. It infused him with heat and accelerated his pulse. Once again she placed her fingers against his lips.

She leaned so close to him he was surrounded by

her scent and could see his own reflection in the shiny depths of her dark-brown eyes. "And your problem with that would be?"

Before he had an opportunity to reply, motion out of the corner of his eye drew his attention. At a nearby table, the familiar blond-haired man stood, a camera up to his face.

Farid sprang into action, his stomach knotted with rage. In four long strides he was before the man. He grabbed the camera.

"Hey! What in the hell do you think you're doing?" the man demanded as Farid ripped open the back of the camera to expose the film.

"I'm helping you with your processing," he said tersely as he pulled the film completely out.

The camera was a professional one, and he spied the notepad and pen peeking out of the man's breast pocket. A reporter. He should have known. Dammit, he should have paid more attention when he'd first had a bad feeling about the man.

"You can't do that," the man exclaimed in obvious outrage.

"I just did." Farid set the camera on the table, then turned and walked back to Samira, who had risen from the table with a hand across her mouth.

"The public has a right to know about Princess Samira's activities," the man yelled to them. "Princess…how about an interview? What are you doing here in Montebello and who is the creep who just screwed up my pictures?"

"Come on, let's get out of here," Farid said, aware

that they had drawn the interested gazes of the people around them. He grabbed her by the arm and together they left the patio area.

"What was that all about?" she asked.

"I'm pretty sure the man was paparazzi. I saw him snapping a picture of us together."

She shot him a worried glance. "He recognized me."

"Yes, apparently he did."

Her frown deepened. "I can just see the headline that might have accompanied our photo in one of the tabloids. Bodyguard or Lover?" She sighed miserably.

He squeezed her arm. "Don't worry, there won't be a photograph from that particular roll of film."

She nodded and they walked for a little while in silence. "I wonder how many other photos he might have taken of us over the last week or so?"

"I don't know." Anger coursed through him once again. He should have confronted the man that day on the beach, when he'd had the feeling that he was following them. "It's my fault," he said, his anger evident in his voice. "I should have been paying more attention."

"It's not your fault," she protested. "And in any case, there wasn't much you could do about it.

"It's time to go home, isn't it Farid?" she finally asked in a small voice.

"Yes, Princess. I think it's time we go home." Farid felt the weight of depression settling over his shoulders.

He knew their return to Tamir would, in all probability, mark the end of his duty where Samira was concerned. And he also knew that their return to Tamir would mark the beginning of the end of their marriage.

Desmond stroked a hand up Ursula's naked hip, fighting the anger that had grown with each day that had passed. They had just indulged in a rowdy bout of lovemaking, and more than once during the act Desmond had had to stifle his impulse to wrap his hands around her slender neck and squeeze until she breathed no more.

For over two weeks she'd been dangling her secret before him like a coveted carrot. He'd wined and dined her, played the role of besotted lover and now his patience had reached an end.

He had also learned only that morning that Samira was here in Montebello, staying in one of the guest cottages, but he had yet to find a minute to himself in order to see her. Ursula had been like his shadow, constantly in his face since the moment she'd arrived. If he could escape Ursula's presence for just a few minutes, he intended to find Samira and hedge his bet with the lovely princess.

As if she sensed his restlessness, she raised her head from his chest and looked at him. She didn't look so attractive now, with her eye makeup smeared beneath her eyes and her lipstick gone altogether.

"That was wonderful, lover," she said, her voice

throaty like a contented cat's purr. "Was it good for you?"

"You know it was," he said dryly. Sex with Ursula was always good. She was an adventurous, uninhibited lover who knew how to please a man.

She smiled at him, then sat up. "I'll be right back."

With the unselfconsciousness of a very young child, she got up from the bed and padded naked into the bathroom. As she closed the door behind her, Desmond got out of the bed and pulled on a pair of boxers.

Resentment clawed at him as he went to the nearby portable bar and poured himself a healthy dose of scotch. He took a drink and returned to the bed with glass in hand.

Things were getting worse as far as Desmond's position in the royal family. Too many meetings were taking place behind closed doors, meetings between key players of power.

Since Prince Lucas's return to Montebello, Desmond had felt himself being systematically squeezed out of all palace affairs, and he didn't like it. He didn't like it one damn bit.

And the bitch in the bathroom had played him long enough. If she didn't spill her secret tonight, then he was done with her. He still had his ace in the hole...the lovely Princess Samira, although he was beginning to become concerned because he hadn't been able to get in touch with her for almost three weeks.

Still, if things didn't go well here and he found

himself completely on the outs, he would marry Samira and move to Tamir. In that small country he would find a way to ingratiate himself with the Kamal family.

He took another drink of his scotch and settled back against the thick pillows as Ursula came out of the bathroom. She was now clad in his white terry robe and she'd washed her face and applied fresh makeup.

She sauntered over to the bar and poured herself a glass of champagne from the bottle he'd opened earlier. As she walked back to the bed she trailed her fingers across the top of his dresser, touching a bottle of his cologne, then the marble base of a statuette of a naked woman that had caught his fancy.

"A toast," she said as she rejoined him on the bed. She held her glass out toward him. "To our future, may it be as glorious as I think it's going to be."

He held his glass against his chest and said nothing.

She frowned. "What's wrong? You aren't going to toast to our future?"

"I'm not sure we *have* a future," he replied.

"What do you mean?" Her frown deepened.

He took another sip of his scotch, enjoying the slight burn of the alcohol down his throat. It distracted him momentarily from his building rage. "I mean that it's obvious you're either playing games with me or you don't trust me, and in either case that doesn't exactly speak well for us having any sort of future together."

She quickly set her glass on the nightstand next to

the bed, then turned back to him, her expression holding an edge of fear. "I'm sorry, sweetheart. You're right, I've been bad."

She moved closer to him and placed a hand on his chest. "I just wanted to spend some time with you, I wanted us to have some time together before things get crazy."

Amazement shot through Desmond. The poor bitch fancies herself in love with me, he thought in surprise. Power surged through his veins as he realized he'd made yet another conquest.

Still he remained silent, utilizing the silence as a tool of displeasure. He could tell it worked when she sat up and grabbed her glass of champagne.

She took a sip, put the glass back on the stand, then draped herself across him, her head on his chest and her hand once again caressing through the dark hairs on his chest.

"What do you think it would be worth to the person who could deliver a new heir to Montebello?" she asked.

Desmond shoved her up off his chest, adrenaline pumping through him at her words. He stared at her in bewilderment. "What are you talking about? What new heir?"

Ursula tucked a strand of her tawny blond hair behind her ear and once again left the bed. She grabbed her glass of champagne, then walked across the bedroom floor and sat in the brocade chair opposite the bed. "You know that while Prince Lucas was suffering amnesia he worked as a ranch hand on my sister's place in Colorado.''

''I know that,'' Desmond replied impatiently.

She took a sip of her champagne, then smiled at him. ''But did you know that Prince Lucas and my sister, Jessica, were lovers?'' She shook her head. ''Poor Jessica, she was so smitten she didn't even think about birth control. And she had no idea she was sleeping with a crown prince. She thought she was sleeping with a down-and-out cowhand named Joe.''

Desmond sat up and placed his glass on the night-stand as the implication of her words sank in. ''Your sister is pregnant with Prince Lucas's child?'' He swung his legs over the edge of the bed and faced her, his blood pumping as hot in his veins as if he were about to have sex.

''Not anymore. I'm saddened to report that two days after I arrived here in Montebello, my poor sister died after giving birth to a healthy son.'' The glitter in her bright blue eyes belied any sadness she might pretend at her sister's passing.

''A healthy son? Prince Lucas's child?'' Desmond stood and grabbed Ursula's hand and pulled her back on the bed with him. ''Why haven't I heard anything about this? No whispers? No rumors? Are you sure the child is his?''

''Positive. Prince Lucas left the ranch before he knew of Jessica's condition. He has no idea he's a daddy. Nobody knows there is a child.''

He could be a hero again. The knowledge sang

through Desmond's veins. He could unite Prince Lucas with his son, give the king and queen their grandson and they would be forever in his debt.

"You have to tell me everything, Ursula. This is far too important to screw up. I need to know where the baby is now and I need to know exactly what happened to your sister."

Ursula's features hardened. "Jessica was being a total fool. When she realized that Joe was really the crown prince of Montebello, she refused to use the baby as a pawn. She was in the way of my future."

A faint chill sliced through Desmond as he stared at her.

"How did your sister die, Ursula?"

"How would I know? I wasn't there," she answered flippantly.

He grabbed her wrist in a tight vise grip. "Don't play games with me. I told you I need to know everything."

She wrenched her wrist from his grip and rubbed it, giving him a wounded look. "All right, all right. I don't know all the details, I left those up to Gretchen."

"Gretchen?"

She nodded. "Gretchen Hanson. She and I have been friends since we were kids. Gretchen's life hasn't exactly been a piece of cake. Since she was twenty and her parents died in an accident, she's been stuck taking care of her idiot brother."

"Idiot brother?"

She nodded. "Yeah, Gerald. He's thirty-three and

simpleminded. He does odd jobs around Shady Rock, but he's always been a ball and chain around Gretchen's ankles.''

"So, what do this Gretchen and her stupid brother have to do with all this?" Desmond asked with a renewed burst of impatience.

"Gretchen is a midwife and, like me, she's hungry for more than life has given her.'' Ursula got up and poured herself some more champagne, then returned to the bed next to Desmond.

"I had a little savings put away and I promised it to her if she saw to it that baby Luke was born healthy and Jessica didn't survive the birth.''

She'd arranged her own sister's death. Amazement washed over Desmond as he recognized the extent of Ursula's ambition. The only other person he'd ever known in his life to possess such ambition and drive was himself.

"Jessica died, and Gretchen had Gerald dispose of the body. With the money I gave her, she intends to institutionalize Gerald so she can finally have a life of her own.''

Desmond didn't give a damn about some midwife and her simpleton relative. "Where is the baby now? How soon can we get him here?''

"Gretchen is just awaiting my phone call and for arrangements to be made for her to travel with baby Luke.''

Desmond picked up the telephone and placed it between them on the mattress. "Then call her now and

I'll see to it that plane tickets are awaiting her first thing in the morning.''

Ursula smiled, the self-satisfied smile of a cat who'd just dined on a canary. "This is it, isn't it, Desmond? What we need to get what we want.''

He picked up the phone receiver and handed it to her. "Make the call, Ursula. This is definitely the break we've been waiting for.''

When the call had been made and the arrangements confirmed, Desmond drew Ursula into his arms. The irritation that had burned inside him for the past two weeks was gone, usurped by the rush of the anticipation of success.

"Do you have any idea what that little baby is worth?'' he asked as he pulled his robe from her. "Prince Lucas's son...King Marcus and Queen Gwendolyn's second grandson. The son of the king's heir.''

"And I'm his auntie...the only relative from the Chambers side of the family. I foresee myself in an intimate position of favor with the royal family.'' She stretched languidly against him, her eyes glowing like a feline's.

He raked a finger across her lower lip, watching as the glow in her eyes grew brighter. "And it was right of you to come to me with this information. When the child arrives here in Montebello, I will see to it that you have a private audience with the royal family to deliver the good news.''

She drew his finger into her mouth, then released

it. "And to celebrate, I think we should go out tonight, eat dinner at the Glass Swan."

"All right," he agreed. Why not? It seemed fitting that he take her out for one last good meal, because once he had that baby he wouldn't need her anymore.

Poor Ursula. She had no idea that she wouldn't be alive to see a king's ransom.

He wasn't about to share the glory of reuniting Prince Lucas with his infant son with a two-bit actress and a midwife. There was a part of him that admired Ursula's ruthlessness, but her ruthlessness didn't begin to compare to his own.

Chapter 9

"I'm glad we decided to come here for dinner," Samira said to Farid, who sat across the table from her in the Glass Swan Restaurant.

They were seated next to the large windows that offered a view of the harbor, and they had just placed their dinner orders with the waitress.

"At least we're here early enough to beat the dinner rush," he said.

She smiled at him. "Yes, heaven forbid we should have to wait for a table." In the two weeks that they'd been married, she'd discovered that Farid had little patience with standing in line when it came to his meals.

He returned her smile. "At least it doesn't take me ten minutes to decide on what I want to order."

"I can't help it if it takes me a while to make up my mind."

"And I suppose you also can't help it that you're a bed hog." His eyes teased with her and she felt heat leap into her cheeks.

He was right. She was a bed hog. Every morning she awakened on his side of the bed, wrapped in his big strong arms. And every morning she'd wished he would kiss her...stroke his hands down the length of her, make love to her again, but he didn't.

"We won't talk about your snoring," she returned.

"I don't snore," he protested with a grin.

"Then we need to lock up better at night because if it isn't you, then somebody is sneaking into our room and cutting Z's."

He laughed and once again she felt warmth, only this time it didn't heat her cheeks, but rather warmed her heart. They sounded like a real married couple, and she was beginning to feel like one.

The past week had brought a new intimacy to their relationship even though they had not made love again. She knew he liked his toast unbuttered and his socks one-hundred percent cotton. She knew he shaved twice a day, morning and before bed, and didn't like to talk before he had his first cup of coffee in the morning.

But, more than that, she'd learned that any mention of his mother brought a mysterious, profound darkness to his eyes, that he seemed to revel in talking about the baby she carried and that there was a part of himself she sensed that he kept guarded.

"We need to be at the airport by around nine this evening. The jet will be ready to leave immediately," he said. His expression was one of concern. "Will you be all right to travel that late?"

"Yes, although I'll probably nap on the plane." She tried to ignore the apprehension that tightened her stomach as she thought of returning to Tamir and breaking the news of her marriage and her pregnancy to her parents. She looked at her watch. It was just a little after four. "At least that will give us lots of time to shower and pack before we have to leave. I've already thanked Queen Gwendolyn and King Marcus for their hospitality when I spoke to them this afternoon and told them we were going home this evening."

He nodded and took a drink of his water. He set the glass down and looked at her. "Samira, when you make a promise to somebody do you keep it no matter what?"

His voice was suddenly solemn and she looked at him in surprise. "Of course. I take my promises quite seriously. Why?"

"I want you to make a promise to me."

"What?" Something about his expression caused the anxiety to renew itself in her chest.

"I want you to promise me that no matter what you won't tell your father the truth about your pregnancy, that you will let him think the child is mine until we agree to say differently."

His gaze was dark, unfathomable, and Samira wished their intimacy was such that she could guess at his inner thoughts. But she couldn't. "Why do you want me to promise that?" she asked.

"My reasons aren't important...just promise me that you won't say anything until we talk about it."

"All right," she agreed. "I promise."

He visibly relaxed and she wondered what had prompted him to request such a thing. Again worry fluttered through her as she anticipated their return to Tamir.

He reached out across the table and lightly touched the back of her hand. "It's going to be all right. I promise you that everything is going to be fine."

She smiled, strangely comforted by his words and the fact that although it was rare that she could guess at his thoughts, he seemed to be growing more adept at guessing hers.

"And you always keep your promises?" she asked.

"Always," he replied.

At that moment the waitress arrived with their meal and Samira found herself relaxing once again as Farid entertained her with stories of his early days working palace security.

She wasn't sure if the stories he told her were true, but he made her laugh and took her mind off the return home later that night.

There were moments when she gazed at him across the table and couldn't believe that he was her husband. She wondered if she would ever tire of looking at him. Somehow she didn't think so.

Each time she studied his face she saw something new and fascinating there. A mole just beneath his chin, a faint scar at the edge of his right eyebrow…each and every new discovery was like a gift, and she reveled in each one.

They finished their meal but lingered over dessert as if reluctant to bring to an end their last evening together in Montebello.

As she ate a spoonful of chocolate mousse, she was struck with a longing so intense it stunned her.

It was a longing to be held by Farid, to have him kiss her again as passionately as he had that night a week before. A sweet, aching desire fluttered through her.

She wanted him again. She wanted to make love with him, but she didn't know how to show him, how to tell him of her desire for him.

What was worse was the fear that he would abide by her wishes and make love to her, not because he particularly wanted to, but because it was his duty.

She dabbed her napkin to her lips, feeling overly warm with the heat of her thoughts. "If you'll excuse me, I'd like to go to the ladies' room," she said.

He rose as she did and she waved her hands dismissively. "Farid, the restrooms are within sight of this table. It isn't necessary for you to accompany me."

He frowned and remained standing as she left the table. She was aware of his gaze on her as she made her way to the restrooms in the back.

Once inside the ladies' room, she wet a towel and slid it over her cheeks. It was refreshingly cool, but did little to douse the fire that had ignited in the pit of her stomach.

She had been able to excuse their lovemaking before. They had momentarily lost control. It had been a natural curiosity that needed to be satisfied.

So why did she want it again? Why was she so eager to change the rules of their marriage? Maybe she wasn't the good and dutiful daughter she'd always believed herself to be. Maybe there was a streak of wicked wantonness in her.

Once again she drew the cool towel over her fevered cheeks and brow. Was it wanton and wicked to want the man you were married to?

You don't love one another, a little voice whispered in her head. She eyed her reflection in the mirror, irritated with her desire and her doubts.

She tossed the towel into the trash receptacle, then left the restroom—and bumped directly into Desmond Caruso.

She froze, for a moment unable to move as they stood face-to-face with one another.

"Samira!" He took her by the shoulders, his face radiating his shock. "My dear, what a surprise! I've been trying for the past several weeks to get in touch with you. Why didn't you tell me you were coming here to Montebello?"

"Let me go, Desmond," she said stiffly.

"Let you go? Darling, I don't want to let you go. I've missed you so much."

How could she have ever believed herself in love with this man? she wondered. She'd once thought him so handsome, but now she realized his smile was too smooth, the cleft in his chin too pronounced, and his eyes radiated nothing resembling warmth.

"Yes, I'm sure you've just been locked in your room, pining away for me since the last time we were together," she said dryly.

She tried to twist away from beneath his hands, but he tightened his grip. "You're angry with me." He shot a quick glance to a nearby table where a blond-haired woman was seated with her back to them. Samira suspected it was the same blonde she'd seen through his living-room window the night she'd come to surprise him with her news.

"Just let go of me," she repeated angrily.

"Not until you tell me where you're staying. I'll come to you later and we'll talk."

"I believe the lady asked you to let her go." Farid's deep voice boomed from behind Samira.

"Go away and mind your own business," Desmond snapped, not taking his eyes off Samira.

Farid pulled her from Desmond's grip and placed an arm around her shoulder. "You don't understand. Samira is my business."

Farid's voice was taut, filled with a simmering anger that portended danger, but Desmond seemed utterly oblivious to the threat.

He grinned, an ugly grin that transformed his features from handsome to unattractive as his gaze went from Samira to Farid, then back again. "Ah, I see...so that's the way it is. The little princess has taken on a new lover." He laughed, an offensive sound that sickened Samira.

He directed his gaze to Farid. "You should thank me, hero. I broke her in for you, although I must confess, she was a lousy lay."

Samira gasped as Farid exploded from her side. He slammed Desmond up against the wall, his big hand wrapped around Desmond's throat.

Somebody from a table nearby yelled out and a woman screamed. Samira watched in horror as Desmond reached up in an unsuccessful attempt to pull Farid's hand from his neck. "Let me go," he choked.

"If you ever touch her again…if you ever talk about her like that again…I'll kill you." Farid's voice seethed with rage. "Do you hear me, Caruso? I will not tolerate you disrespecting her. If you do it again, I'll hunt you down and kill you."

Abruptly he released his hold on Desmond, who stumbled and knocked into a nearby table, overturning glasses as the diners at that particular table jumped up in horror.

Farid grabbed Samira's arm and together they walked toward the restaurant door. They were followed to the door by a hand-wringing Louis Montague. Montague was the owner of the restaurant and obviously disturbed by the fracas that had just occurred.

"I apologize for the disturbance," Farid said to Louis when they reached the front of the restaurant. He pulled out several bills and offered them to Louis. "For any damage that might have occurred."

Louis waved the money away, then tugged on his dark goatee. "I apologize that one of my guests showed an incredible lack of breeding in saying such things to a lady."

Samira wanted to die as she realized the dapper man had overhead what Desmond had said about her. Tears of humiliation filled her eyes and she clung to Farid's arm, just wanting to leave, to escape from this place.

The walk back to their guest house was accomplished in silence. She could feel Farid's anger still radiating from him, a palpable force like a companion walking with them.

Desmond's vile, ugly words swirled around and around in her head, echoing painfully in her heart. There was no way she could even pretend now that Desmond might have liked her just a little bit.

His words had been demeaning and contemptuous, and she felt like such a fool for ever allowing him to touch her in any way.

When they reached the guest house, Samira went right into the bathroom, telling Farid she wanted to shower. What she really wanted to do was to wash off the feel of Desmond's hands on her shoulders. She felt slimy and dirty from his touch.

As she stood beneath the hot spray of the shower, she wondered how it was possible that she could be so smart in matters of the heart for other people, but so incredibly stupid when it came to her own life.

Others often came to her for advice about their romances. She'd even been instrumental in helping her

brother Hassan understand what he needed to do to
win over the woman he loved. So, why was she so
incredibly naïve? Why had she been so vulnerable to
a man like Desmond?

A lousy lay. The words had been low-class and
meant to hurt. But now, Samira wondered if perhaps
that's why Farid hadn't tried to make love to her
again after the first time. She'd been so bad at it, he
hadn't been able to force himself to touch her again.

A wave of deep despair swept through her and she
wept, knowing the sounds of her sobs would be swallowed by the sound of the shower.

He'd wanted to kill him. Rage still ripped through
Farid as his mind filled with a vision of Samira's
stricken face. He'd never wanted to hurt anyone as
badly as he'd wanted to hurt Desmond Caruso.

Even now his fists ached with the need to smash
Caruso's pretty-boy face. He wanted to make it impossible for Samira's name to ever again fall out of
Desmond's mouth. He couldn't remember the last
time he'd felt such rage. Certainly he'd never felt this
kind of anger over a woman.

With the sound of Samira taking a shower in the
next room, Farid walked over to the bar and poured
himself a shot of whisky.

It had been bad enough that Caruso had placed his
hands on her, but the foul words that had left his
mouth had made Farid see red.

He downed the jigger of whisky, then poured himself another one and sank down on the sofa. Slowly

the raging adrenaline that had filled him dissipated, leaving behind an ache in his heart for Samira.

When Desmond had said those ugly things, the look on her face had been devastating. She'd lost all color in her cheeks and her hands had flown to her stomach as if she would shield her unborn child from the man who was the father.

He'd wanted to shield not only the baby, but Samira herself from Desmond. But he knew that while he'd been able to remove Samira from Desmond's presence tonight, he wouldn't always be able to do so.

For at least the next eighteen years, Desmond Caruso would always have a place in Samira's life because of the child they shared.

And while Farid wished it wasn't so, there was no way he could change the fact that Desmond Caruso was the biological father of Samira's child and as such he would have to be afforded certain rights.

The sound of the shower ceased. He frowned and sipped his drink, relishing the burn of the alcohol down his throat. He worried about what was going through Samira's pretty little head. He knew how much she hated confrontation, and he'd certainly been a party to causing a huge showdown.

The entire congregation in the restaurant had been witness not only to her humiliation, but also to the violent scene Farid had caused.

He turned as the bedroom door opened and she came out. Clad in a short, pale-pink terry robe, she looked small and achingly vulnerable.

He motioned her to sit next to him on the sofa and when she did, his senses were filled with the clean, sweet scent of her. Her hair was damp and clung to her neck, and without any makeup on she looked younger than her years.

Her eyes were reddened and he realized she'd been crying. Although she was seated next to him, she refused to meet his gaze. Her fingers worried with the fringe at the ends of the belt that cinched the robe at her waist.

Was she angry with him for losing control and making a small scene into a bigger scene? He finished his drink and set his empty glass on the coffee table before them.

"Samira...I'm sorry."

Her deep-brown eyes looked up at him in surprise. "For what?"

"For making such a scene."

She once again looked down at her hands, the belt still entwined in her fingers. "There's nothing to apologize for. It wasn't your fault." She shivered slightly. "He was awful and it was all his fault."

"Yes, but I lost my temper. I lost control and that's something I try never to do."

"So, you lost control. It was no big deal." She continued to look down. "I wouldn't have minded if you'd hit him once or twice just for good measure."

He wondered if she were naked beneath the robe. If he slipped the terry material off one shoulder, would he be greeted by the straps of a gown beneath or would there only be her smooth, sweet skin?

The thought of her naked filled him with heat and he cursed himself for being an insensitive bastard. She had just been through an unsettling experience and all he could think about was capturing her lips with his, cupping her breasts with his hands and burying himself deep inside her.

All thoughts of anything sexual instantly left him as she looked up at him, her eyes awash with tears. The misery that reflected from the watery depths of her gentle brown eyes stirred a deep protectiveness he'd never known before.

He pulled her into his arms and she came willingly, wrapping her arms around his neck and burying her face in the front of his shirt. "I can't believe I ever let that man touch me in any way," she said, her voice muffled against his chest. "I can't believe I ever believed anything that fell out of his ugly mouth."

"You don't have to worry about that ever again," Farid replied, stroking a hand down her still-damp hair. The pleasant scent of her floral shampoo filled his nose and again a wave of desire swept through him.

"He's a mean, hateful man with a black, black heart and I hate him."

Farid didn't reply, but merely tightened his arms around her.

At least she wasn't crying, he thought. Apparently all she needed was to be held, and he could do that gladly. Holding Samira was remarkably easy to do.

Minutes ticked by and he felt her slowly relaxing against him. Neither of them spoke but the silence wasn't unpleasant. After several minutes had passed, he began to wonder if perhaps she'd fallen asleep, but then she convulsed against him and released a deep, wrenching sob.

"Samira? Why are you crying?" he asked, wondering what had brought on the belated burst of tears. "Tell me what's wrong."

She shook her head and kept her face buried against his chest. "I don't think I want to talk about it," she said through her tears.

Was it possible she was crying from a broken heart? That somehow she'd entertained some kind of lingering hope about a relationship with Desmond Caruso, a hope that had been irrevocably dashed tonight?

"Samira, honey…don't cry." He patted her back, unsure what else to do. Farid didn't know how to deal with a sobbing woman.

"I…can't…help…it." Her shoulders shook with the force of the sobs that ripped through her. She raised her head and looked at him and never had he seen such abject misery on a face. "I know now why you haven't made love to me in the last week. It's because I'm…a…lousy…lay."

Without warning she jumped out of his embrace and off the sofa, then turned and raced for the bedroom. Astonishment momentarily left Farid inert, incapable of movement of any kind.

That's why she was crying? Not because her heart was broken by Desmond but because she'd believed the crazy words he'd said about her lovemaking? She had taken his foolish, hurtful words to heart?

She really believed that Farid had not made love to her after the first time because the experience had been an unpleasant one?

How on earth could she believe that? Hadn't she seen his desire for her in his eyes, felt it in his touch? Didn't she realize how much he wanted her?

His incredulity passed and he jumped up off the sofa and entered the bedroom, where she was on her tummy on the bed, her face buried in a pillow.

The room was falling into purple shadows of approaching twilight and she looked heartbreakingly tiny in the middle of the king-size bed.

He stretched out next to her on the bed and placed a hand on the small of her back, touched by how fragile she felt and vowing that no matter what happened in their future he would do his best to never allow anyone to harm her. It didn't matter whether their marriage lasted or not...he would always want to keep her from hurt...from harm.

"Samira, my sweet, innocent Samira, surely you can't really believe what Caruso said about you."

"Why shouldn't I believe it?" she asked, her voice muffled by the pillow. "We haven't...you haven't tried to even touch me in that way since that one time."

"And you have no idea how difficult it has been for me not to touch you in 'that way' since the last time we made love."

"You're just saying that," she replied.

"Trust me, Samira, I'm not just saying that. A few minutes ago while I was holding you in my arms, I was wondering if you were naked beneath your robe. I was imagining kissing you again, caressing you again...making love to you again."

She raised her face from the pillow and looked at him. Her cheeks were stained with the tracks of her tears and her bottom lip quivered with barely suppressed emotion.

"You're just being nice," she protested.

"You know me better than that," he chided gently. "I never do anything just to be nice." He reached out a finger and stroked it down her cheek, swiping away an errant tear that lingered there.

"You have no idea how much I've wanted you this past week," he said softly. "I wake up in the morning hard and throbbing with my desire for you, and I go to sleep at night the same way. I watch you shopping in the piazza and I want to make love to you. I see you sitting in a restaurant opposite me and I want to make love to you. The night that we made love, I found you to be a beautiful, passionate lover that I instantly wanted again...and again."

"Then why haven't you tried to make love to me again?" she asked, her voice slightly breathless.

"Because I didn't want to do anything that you didn't want me to. But, trust me, Samira, not a minute has gone by that I haven't been half-crazed with wanting you." He didn't wait for her to reply, but leaned forward and captured her lips with his.

The gentle kiss he'd meant to give her instantly

raged into something more as she wound her arms around his neck and pulled him more intimately against her.

She returned his kiss with a fevered hunger that sent desire crashing through his veins. Their tongues battled in an erotic dance that merely heightened his passion for her.

"Farid." She tore her mouth from his, her eyes glowing in the semidarkness of the room. "I am."

He frowned down at her, finding thought next to impossible. "You are what?"

She smiled, a sexy smile that sent rivulets of electricity tingling through him. "I am naked beneath this robe."

For the second time in twenty-four hours, Farid lost complete control.

Chapter 10

As Farid removed the robe from her, kissing each inch of skin as it was exposed, all thoughts of Desmond and his mean words faded from her mind.

When Farid touched her, when he kissed her, it was impossible to think of anything but him and the wonderful, exciting sensations he evoked in her.

When her robe was gone, thrown to the floor next to the bed, he got up only long enough to remove his clothing, then rejoined her.

"Never doubt how much I desire you," he said just before his mouth claimed hers in a hot, hungry kiss.

And she didn't. She couldn't doubt his desire when it was so evident. She not only felt it, hard and throbbing against her, she also tasted it in his kiss, felt it radiating through his fingertips.

It was difficult for a man to fake desire, much easier for a woman to do so. She had faked it with Desmond to please him, but she didn't have to fake anything with Farid.

As his mouth left hers and traveled down the length of her neck, and his hands cupped her breasts, she gasped with pleasure.

She tangled her fingers in his thick black hair, lost in sensual splendor as his mouth reached where his hands were and his tongue teased first one nipple, then the other. She felt as if her breasts were electrified and each time he touched them currents of energy coursed throughout her entire body.

''Never doubt that I want to make love to you anytime, anyplace,'' he murmured. ''You positively enflame me with desire for you.''

She wasn't sure if it was his words that moved her or his continued caressing of her, but tension began to build inside her, a tension that was both frightening and wonderful.

One of his hands left her breasts and trailed down her rib cage, caressing her hip, her inner thigh, but not touching her where she needed him most.

He raised his head and looked at her, his eyes glittering with a ferocious hunger. ''It has been sheer torture, lying next to you each night in bed and not touching you.''

''You should have touched me,'' she said, gasping with the effort of trying to speak while her heart pounded frantically and her pulse raced erratically.

"You should have reached out for me. I would have come to you willingly, eagerly."

"I didn't want to offend you," he replied.

"This doesn't offend me, this electrifies me."

Once again his fingers moved up the sensitive skin of her inner thigh, stopping just short of touching her intimately. It was a sensual, heart-stopping form of torture that merely served to heighten both her frustration and her utter pleasure.

She wanted to give him the same kind of fevered sensations that he was giving her. With this thought in mind, she sat up and pushed him to his back.

Her fingers trembled as she ran them across the broad expanse of his chest. His heartbeat thundered beneath her fingertips and she leaned down and placed her lips on the spot where she thought his heart might be.

Moving her hands down the flat of his stomach, she felt his swift intake of breath as she avoided touching him as he had done to her.

She touched his inner thighs where she knew the skin was sensitive and a low moan escaped him and she felt the tension that surged in his body.

"Samira." His voice held both an unspoken warning and a plea.

"Farid." She answered her name with his own and smiled, reveling in the knowledge that she was giving to him the same kind of pleasure he'd given to her.

She wrapped her fingers around him and heard the hiss of his swift intake of breath. She was surprised to discover that his obvious pleasure at her touch increased her own.

She stroked her hand down the length of him, but before she could repeat the motion, he rolled her on her back beneath him.

"Are you trying to drive me insane?" he asked, his voice filled with an urgency that thrilled her.

"Yes...I want you insane with wanting me," she replied.

"Then you have succeeded, my love," he said, then crushed his mouth to hers for a kiss that stole all reason from her mind.

He eased into her, filling her up with his heat and she welcomed him, arching up and wrapping her hands around his back.

The mind-blowing sensations that soared through her half-blinded her and she closed her eyes, allowing herself to wallow in the flames of fire that filled her.

He buried himself deep within her, then pulled back until he was barely touching her. She gripped his buttocks, and pulled him back deeply into her, crying out as he once again nearly withdrew.

The teasing strokes drove her half-wild and she cried out in both frustration and ecstasy. As if her cry had broken loose something inside him, he changed the rhythm to a frenzied pace that took her breath away.

Faster and faster they moved together and the explosion of her release shuddered through her with an intensity that left her mindless.

His body went taut as a bow string and he stiffened

against her, emitting a groan of pure, unadulterated pleasure with his own release.

For a long moment he remained unmoving, the bulk of his weight held off her by his arms on either side of her. Even in the near-darkness of the room she could see his eyes gazing at her. They were filled with a tenderness that surprised her, yet warmed her.

He leaned down and gave her a gentle, lingering kiss that stirred her as deeply, as profoundly as what they'd just shared. She wondered how she'd ever been able to think of this man as cold and arrogant.

He rolled over to the side of her and drew her into his arms. She curled her body next to his, her hand on his chest where his heartbeat was beginning to slow to a more normal pace.

"There's only one reason why I haven't made love to you in this past week," he said, his voice deep and soft.

She raised her head to look at him, loving the way the moonlight played across his strong features. "And why is that?"

"Because I didn't want to break the rule that you set down when we married."

She smiled and stroked a hand through the tuft of hair that decorated the center of his chest. "It was a foolish rule."

"I won't disagree with that," he replied and tightened his arm around her.

"I wish I could sleep in your arms tonight, Farid."

He smiled, that slow, sexy grin that created a new

burst of heat through her. "You can sleep in my arms on the plane tonight."

"Then tomorrow night I'll sleep in your arms in our bed," she said, the thought shooting a new burst of warmth through her. She slid from his arms and sat up, eyeing the clock on the nightstand next to him. "I need to go pack up the last of my things in the bathroom."

He nodded and she felt his gaze on her as she left the bed, picked up her robe from the floor and walked to the bathroom. Once in the privacy of the master bath, she stared at her reflection in the mirror.

Her hair was tousled and her cheeks were filled with color. Her lips were slightly swollen and she looked as if she'd just been thoroughly and completely loved.

As she had been. Happiness soared through her as she thought of Farid's passion, how sweetly he had made her body sing in response.

She may be relatively inexperienced, but she knew instinctively that Farid was a wonderful lover. It had been foolish of her to believe they could live a life together, share the intimacies of marriage, yet not share a physical relationship.

She would have been denying herself incredible pleasure in denying them a physical intimacy. She also knew now that there was no going back. From here on out their marriage would be a real one, including frequent lovemaking.

Pulling on her robe, then a pair of panties, she realized that in the past two and a half weeks that they had been in Montebello, her tummy had grown more pronounced.

A new thought shot a touch of fear through her. Would Farid still want her when her stomach bulged and her ankles swelled with her pregnancy? Would he still desire her when she was fat and pregnant, or would he find her repulsive?

It took her only minutes to pack her toiletries into a small suitcase. When she returned to the bed, Farid was lying on his back, his arms behind his head.

He motioned for her to rejoin him. "We still have a little time before we have to get up," he said. As she got into the bed next to him he once again placed an arm around her and pulled her against his side.

His hand stroked her shoulder and although she tried to relax, she couldn't with the weight of her worry on her heart. She raised her head and gazed at him.

He touched the tip of her nose with his index finger. "What's wrong? I see a frown."

"I was just wondering if you won't want me anymore when my belly gets big and fat."

He sat up, his features registering surprise. "Is that what you're worried about? That as your pregnancy advances suddenly I won't want you anymore?"

To her surprise, he pushed up her robe to expose her tummy. Placing a hand against the tiny bulge, his gaze held hers. "I'm going to want every ounce, every pound of weight that you gain. I'm going to find you beautiful and desirable as the baby grows inside you."

He leaned down and kissed her lower abdomen and tears of happiness momentarily filled Samira's eyes. Gently, he pulled her robe back down and once again drew her into his embrace against his side. "For as long as you want me, Samira, I'll want you."

She released a sigh of contentment and snuggled against him, loving the feel of their bodies so close together. She knew that all too quickly it would be time for them to get dressed and go to the airport, where the jet would be ready for take-off.

And in all probability within the next twelve to fourteen hours, she would have to face her father. Her mind replayed the scene in the restaurant and again she berated herself for being such a fool where Desmond was concerned.

"Samira, we'd better get up. A car will be here in just a few minutes to take us to the airport."

Reluctantly she once again left his arms. They both got out of bed and dressed in silence. Samira felt as if a magical time in her life was coming to an end. She only hoped the future they faced together would be as magical as these past few days with him.

They were ready and waiting when one of the royal limos pulled up to take them to the airport.

When they were ensconced in the back of the limo, Samira leaned against Farid and sighed. "I'm almost sorry to say goodbye to Montebello," she said. "These last two weeks have been wonderful."

"I've enjoyed spending time with you, Samira."

She sighed once again. "I can't quit thinking about

what a horrid man Desmond is,'' she said. "And what a fool I was to have anything to do with him.''

"Wolves often wear sheep's clothing very well. You need to stop blaming yourself for being a good and trusting human being who got taken advantage of.''

She looked at him gratefully. "You're right,'' she agreed. "But he is vile and hateful and I'm never going to tell him about the baby—never,'' she finished vehemently.

"You're just upset right now,'' Farid replied. "The scene in the restaurant was terrible, but you know that you have to tell Caruso about the baby.''

She moved away from his side and eyed him in surprise. "I know nothing of the kind. I don't *have* to tell him anything.''

"Samira…'' he began.

"I will never let him know that he's the father of my child,'' she exclaimed, interrupting whatever he was about to say. She wasn't sure exactly when she'd made this decision, but she was absolutely, positively adamant about it now.

"Don't be ridiculous,'' he exclaimed.

"Ridiculous?'' She stared at him. "I'm not being ridiculous,'' she protested as she eyed him in amazement.

A darkness had usurped any light in his eyes and he looked frighteningly cold and distant at the moment. "You know what kind of a man Desmond is. I do not want that man in my child's life.''

"You have no right to make a decision like that,''

he replied, his voice tight with an anger that seemed to have sprung from nowhere.

"I have every right," she returned, with a rising anger of her own. "I'm the baby's mother."

"And Desmond is the baby's father and no matter how you wish to change that, you can't. You and Desmond Caruso made a baby together, and Desmond has a right to know that you're going to have his child."

"I don't care. I think I know what's best for my child," she said stiffly.

"Your baby has a right to know its biological father. If you really think that it's best to keep a secret like that then you're a selfish woman thinking only of yourself and your own comfort."

She hadn't even realized they had reached the airport until he opened the car door and got out. He held out a hand to help her out but she ignored it, a seething anger rising up inside her.

What did he know about it, anyway? How dare he accuse her of being selfish? She swept into the jet, aware of Farid just behind her.

How could he be so mean and hateful to her after the tender, beautiful lovemaking they'd shared less than an hour before?

She nodded curtly to the pilot who greeted her, then made her way toward the back of the small luxury jet. There a sitting area awaited her, complete with a buttery-soft leather sofa, a coffee table bearing a fresh-cut floral arrangement and two captain chairs in the same soft gray leather.

She sank down on the sofa. Although she was as angry as she'd ever been with Farid, she was bitterly disappointed when he didn't join her.

In a thousand thoughts, she'd never have dreamed that Farid would feel as strongly as he obviously did, and she hadn't realized until this moment how much she had wanted his support, not his censure.

Was it so selfish to want to protect her child from a man like Desmond Caruso? Was it so horrible to want to keep her child from the influence of a man she knew would not make a good father? He just didn't understand. He couldn't understand how deeply she felt about this particular issue.

Tears oozed from her eyes as she thought of Farid's reaction to her announcement. Would she have to choose between protecting the baby she already loved or pleasing a husband she loved?

She loved Farid? No. Impossible. What she felt for him was gratitude for marrying her...what she felt for him was an incredible physical attraction based on their magnificent lovemaking. But she didn't love him.

Still, this wasn't the way she'd wanted to return to Tamir, with cold words echoing and a chasm of emotional distance between them.

She hated the sick feeling that their confrontation had left in her, hated the coldness that had radiated from his eyes as he'd spoken to her.

Tears once again blurred her vision as she stared out the window, the weight of Farid's disapproval like a stone around her heart.

Swiping the tears from her eyes with the back of one hand, she wondered how they could present a united, loving picture to her parents when they weren't even speaking to one another.

Farid was more angry than he could ever remember being, and he wasn't sure exactly what he was most angry with—the situation, or Samira's apparent ultimate decision, or how both had brought his personal emotional baggage smashing to the forefront.

Samira was making the same selfish decision his mother had made, and Farid recognized that her decision had stirred fires of resentment inside him that really had nothing to do with her.

Samira had no idea of the ramifications of the decision she'd made. She had no idea the harm she would do her child if she denied the child the knowledge of its biological father.

His chest tightened as he thought of his mother's deathbed confession, of all the wasted years, of all the aching loneliness. How on earth could she have kept such a secret from him? How on earth could she have been so damned cruel?

He stared out the window, wishing they were already up in the air. But traveling with a princess required more than just starting up the engines and taking off. Airspace had to be cleared and a military escort needed to be in place.

He eyed his wristwatch. Just before ten. By midnight they would be in Tamir, and in all likelihood, first thing in the morning they would face Sheik Ahmed to tell him their news.

"Farid?"

He turned to see Samira standing in the doorway that separated the two compartments of the small plane. She looked miserable, her eyes holding the residual emotion of their argument. In spite of his anger, he felt a softening as he gazed at her.

"Can we discuss this issue without yelling at one another?"

"I'm not sure," he said honestly.

"Would you come back here and we can try?" Her gentle brown eyes pleaded with him and he couldn't deny her request.

He stood and followed her into the back compartment, where she sat on the sofa and patted the spot next to her.

He sat and stared at the windows opposite them as the jet engines whined and the plane began to move. Within moments they would be in the air.

"Farid, I don't think you really understand that my only motive in not disclosing that Desmond is the father of my baby is to protect my baby."

He directed his gaze to her. "And I don't think you understand that ultimately keeping that secret might very well destroy your child."

He could tell by her expression that she thought his words overly dramatic. As the jet left the ground and ascended into the sky, Farid knew then that it was time for him to tell her about his mother's lies.

Raking a hand through his hair, fighting to suppress

the deep, wrenching emotions that threatened to overwhelm him, he moved to one of the captain chairs facing her.

"My mother lied about who my father was until the day she died," he said without preamble.

Samira's brown eyes stared at him intently. "I don't understand…you said your father was Hashim Nasir and that he died when you were twelve years old."

"That's what I was told until last year when my mother got sick. Then she confessed to me that Hashim Nasir wasn't my biological father." He gazed out the window where there was nothing but darkness, the same kind of darkness he'd felt when Hashim had died.

For him, the sun had stopped shining on the day they had buried Hashim. "I grieved so long and so hard for Hashim," he said aloud, his voice sounding thick and deeper than usual. "And for years I missed his presence in my life—and all the while my mother knew that I had a biological father I could have turned to."

She frowned thoughtfully. "And that knowledge would have taken away your grief at losing Hashim?"

He stared at her in surprise. "Of course not," he exclaimed automatically. And yet, wasn't that what he'd secretly believed? That somehow if he'd known he had a father somewhere else his grief over losing Hashim would have been taken away?

Of course, the idea was utterly ridiculous. Nothing

and nobody could have eased the grief he'd felt over losing Hashim.

He sat forward and once again raked a hand through his hair in perplexity. ''I don't know, maybe I did sort of believe that if I'd known my real father, then I wouldn't have felt such grief over losing Hashim. But that's not true. I loved Hashim.''

''So, who is your real father?''

''His name isn't really important. Apparently he drove through the little village where my mother lived when she was eighteen years old. His car broke down and he came to her house for help. One thing led to another and I was conceived that night. The next morning he was gone.''

''Then your mother married Hashim,'' Samira said.

He nodded. ''She and Hashim had been promised to one another for years. I think they loved each other very much but they had had a fight the day before my real father showed up at my mother's house. Anyway, she never spoke of my real father, never told me the truth about the circumstances of my parentage.''

''Did you ever meet him? Your real father, I mean?'' she asked softly.

''Yeah. When my mother discovered she was so ill, she wrote him a letter, telling him of my existence. The day that she was buried, he came to meet me and we developed a relationship that lasted six months.'' Again pain ripped through his guts. ''Then six months ago he was killed in a car accident.''

He stood, the anger rich and bold inside him. ''Don't you see? She did to me exactly what you want to do to your baby…she deprived me of my real father."

"Farid…" She reached out and took his hand and pulled him down to sit next to her once again. She cupped his face between her hands, her eyes radiating a tenderness that somewhat soothed the beast inside him. "My hearts aches with the losses that you've suffered in your life. You lost not only your mother, but two fathers in the space of one lifetime."

He jerked away from her touch, needing to sustain his anger so that the pain didn't consume him. "She could have made things easier on me if she hadn't kept the secret. I lost years of time with my real father because she was too damned selfish to tell me the truth."

Samira sighed, her gaze troubled as it lingered on him. "Oh, Farid, do you really think it was selfishness that drove your mother?"

He didn't reply…couldn't because of the emotion that clogged his throat. It was a combination of anger and anguish, blended with regrets and recriminations.

Samira grabbed his hand in her small, warm one. "Needless to say, I didn't know your mother, but you said she was a warm, loving person whose family was her priority."

She looked down at the wedding band that circled her ring finger. "The ring is warm, Farid…warm with a mother's love, and I can't imagine that the woman who wore this ring made a decision to intentionally hurt her child. I can't believe her decision was based on anything but tremendous love for you. Do you really, in your heart of hearts, think differently?''

For the first time since his mother's death, for the first time since the startling confession that had brought his real father into his life, Farid was faced with the realization that the mother who had raised him, the mother who had loved him, would have never intentionally hurt him.

The emotions that had moments before been so tight, so suffocating in his chest, broke apart.

''I just wish I'd had more time with my real father,'' he finally said and squeezed Samira's hand in his. He looked at her searchingly. ''I don't want you to make the same mistake my mother did. Don't steal away the relationship between Desmond and your child. You never know what kind of an impact that will have later.''

She nodded almost imperceptibly. ''All right, Farid, when the child is old enough I'll tell him the truth about his father and Desmond can decide then what sort of an influence he will be in his child's life.''

Once again she framed his face with her hands, her eyes so sweet, so gentle he wanted to fall into their depths forever. ''I wish you were the father, Farid.''

Her words, spoken with such heartfelt emotion, shattered the last of any anger he might have about his past, leaving his heart open and vulnerable.

He drew her against his side. She came willingly, snuggling into him as if she belonged with her head against his heart, his chin resting on the top of her head.

He sighed, feeling a helplessness soar through him with every mile that carried them closer to Tamir. He was glad she'd changed her mind about telling the baby about his real father, but she had capitulated to his wishes so easily.

If she wouldn't stand up to him for what she believed to be best for her child, how on earth would she ever stand up to her father if push came to shove?

Chapter 11

Her bedroom.

Always in the past when Samira had entered this room, decorated in sunshine yellow and white with accents of green, she'd felt warm and secure and happy.

Tonight she felt only an abiding loneliness as she looked at the king-size bed where she'd always slept alone and would sleep alone again tonight.

She had tried to talk Farid into staying here with her tonight. After all, they were married and would announce that fact to her parents first thing in the morning.

But, he had insisted that he go to his own quarters, that it would not be right for him to sleep in her room until after they had talked to her parents.

He had left her at the foot of the staircase that led

up to her private quarters, assuring her that he would be at her side in the morning when they met with her parents.

Saarah had laid out Samira's favorite nightgown on the bed and had offered to run a bath, but Samira had sent her away, preferring to be alone.

She now pulled on the nightgown and within minutes was in the big bed alone, wishing Farid was next to her.

Reaching out an arm, she touched the pillow next to hers, wishing Farid's head were resting there. How was it possible that sleeping next to a man for a mere two and a half weeks could create a habit of familiarity that when taken away would cause such a bereavement?

She'd grown accustomed to falling to sleep with the rhythm of Farid's breathing matching her own. She'd grown used to the male scent of him, the warmth that radiated from him. She'd even grown to like the faint snoring that emitted from him early in the morning.

She'd never dreamed she'd desperately miss having him in her bed. She'd never dreamed how quickly he would become such an integral part of her life.

Turning over on her back, she placed her hands on her lower stomach and thought of the baby inside her. Farid's story of his past had illuminated the reasons why he'd been so volatile concerning her initial decision to never tell her baby about Desmond.

Her heart ached for Farid, who had lost years of knowing his real father, but she'd meant what she'd told him. They couldn't begin to guess Raisa's reasons for keeping such a secret from her son, but there was no doubt in Samira's mind that her decision had been based on love for her son.

Samira knew, because she loved her baby and desperately wanted to protect it from harm. She would tell Desmond about his baby…eventually.

Farid was correct. She had no right to keep a father from his child or a child from its father. She could only hope that Desmond would rise to the challenge of being a wonderful, loving, caring influence in the child's life.

And if he couldn't, then she could only hope that she and Farid could counteract any negative influence Desmond might have.

Would she and Farid even be together to accomplish such a lofty goal as to raise a child together? Could they survive as a couple without the kind of love Samira had once dreamed of having? Could they survive years together in a marriage that was based on Farid's duty and her own desperation?

She closed her eyes, drifting to sleep with no answers forthcoming, and awakened with the sun streaming through her windows.

For a moment she was disoriented.

Farid.

Why wasn't he next to her? With his body warming hers? Why weren't his arms around her, holding her tightly against him? Then she remembered they were in the palace in Tamir and she was in the bedroom of her girlhood.

The anxiety that had haunted her each time she'd thought of telling her parents of her pregnancy and her marriage now exploded inside her as she realized the moment was nearly at hand.

Her bedroom door creaked open and Saarah stuck her head in. ''Good morning, Princess.''

Samira forced a smile, although she'd rather bury her head in her pillows and not face the morning to come.

''Would you like me to bring you something from the kitchen or would you prefer I draw you a bath?''

''A bath,'' Samira said. ''And would you get out my silver *jalabiya* with the matching trousers?''

''But of course,'' Saarah replied and disappeared into the bathroom to begin her duties.

Her father liked to see his daughters in traditional clothing and Samira figured she needed every edge she could get when she and Farid told them their news.

Moments later she sank down into the warm, jasmine-scented water in the tub and listened to Saarah as the maid filled her in on the latest palace gossip. As she listened to Saarah's harmless chatter, she tried to calm the nerves that raced through her.

As Saarah helped her dress, the maid didn't mention that Samira had gained weight while on her trip or how snugly the trousers fit around her waist. But Samira saw the light of knowledge in Saarah's dark eyes.

''Thank you, Saarah, that will be all for now,'' Samira said as Saarah finished brushing her hair.

Saarah gave her a respectful bow, then silently left the room. She cast herself one final glance in the mirror, reminding herself that her father obviously liked and trusted Farid, otherwise he would have never appointed Farid her personal bodyguard. Perhaps he would be happy at their union, and all Samira's worries would be for naught.

With this positive thought in mind, she left the wing where her bedroom was located and went downstairs. Farid seemed to appear from nowhere.

"Good morning," he said softly.

He looked as handsome as she'd ever seen him. His navy slacks were sharply pressed, as was his white shirt and navy jacket. He looked crisp and coolly professional, and a small flutter of panic shot through Samira as she felt an emotional distance from him.

Then he smiled and reached out a hand to her. "Are you okay?" he asked. The warmth that radiated from his eyes momentarily banished her nervous tension.

She squeezed his hand. "I am now."

"Your father went into his office a few minutes ago and I believe your mother is in there with him," Farid said.

A new burst of anxiety swept through Samira. "Then I guess it's time to go tell them our news."

Together the two of them walked down the long, grand hallway toward Sheik Ahmed Kamal's private office. Samira's heart thundered so loudly she felt as if it echoed off the walls surrounding them.

Don't be so nervous, she told herself. After all, it was her parents she was about to confront—the mother and father who had loved and nurtured her for all of her life. It wasn't like she was about to face a couple of ogres.

Still, despite the fact that she knew her parents loved her, she also knew how they—well, her father—had reacted to Leila's husband when scandal had forced Leila to marry the man she now loved deeply. Sheik Ahmed now approved of his new son-in-law, but in the beginning things had been a little tense. At least Nadia had just become engaged to a real hero, the man who had exposed her father's former trusted advisor, Butrus Daboir, as a leader of the terrorist group that had caused so much trouble between Tamir and Montebello. The guards on either side of the office door remained unmoving, at attention, as they approached.

Farid released her hand and turned to her. "Samira, remember your promise to me," he murmured as he raised his hand to knock on the door.

She knew the promise he spoke of and nodded, her heart in her throat as his knock was answered by the strong, vibrant voice of her father bidding them entry.

Sheik Ahmed's office was an enormous room, lavishly decorated in rich purples and shining gold accents. Tapestries hung on the walls, depicting the history of Tamir in exquisite needlepoint. Leather chairs and Persian carpets completed the decor.

The focal point of the room was the enormous mahogany desk behind which sat Samira's father.

Samira's mother, Alima, sat in her favorite chair by an arched window that looked out on the ocean, her calendar open on her lap.

Samira knew it was customary for her parents to begin their workday by discussing their individual schedules, and apparently that's just what they had been doing.

As Samira and Farid approached the desk, Alima closed her calendar, set it on the desk and stood, her expression radiating a pleased surprise. "Samira, I didn't realize you had returned from Montebello."

Samira gave her short, slightly plump mother a hug. "We got in very late last night."

Alima hugged her then held her at arm's length. "You look well. Your vacation has agreed with you."

"And things were well in Montebello?" Sheik Ahmed asked.

Samira released her hold on her mother and faced her father.

Sheik Ahmed Kamal was a handsome man with strong features. His hair and beard had, over the years, gone snowy white, merely serving to emphasize the piercing darkness of his intelligent eyes.

"Both King Marcus and Queen Gwendolyn send their regards to you and Mother," she replied. "I enjoyed a nice meal with them and Prince Lucas while I was there."

Sheik Ahmed nodded, his sharp gaze going to Farid, then back to his daughter. "And you needed to bring your bodyguard to bring me their regards? Farid, you enjoyed your time in Montebello?"

"Yes, sir." Farid stepped up to stand next to Samira. Samira wondered if he was as nervous as she was. Certainly he showed no outward sign of nerves.

"Father…we have news to share with you and Mother." Samira's heart banged and her stomach flip-flopped nervously. She drew a deep breath and reached for Farid's hand.

She saw the flare of something in her father's eyes and the surprise that lit her mother's pretty features. "While we were in Montebello, Farid and I were married. We're married and I'm pregnant."

The silence that greeted her announcement was deafening. Samira tightened her grip on Farid's hand as her father stood, his olive skin suddenly flushed an overbright color that portended something bad.

"Ahmed," Alima said softly, as if aware of her husband's thoughts and emotions.

Sickness swooped through Samira as her father walked around his desk and came to stand directly before her and Farid.

There was no mistaking the emotion that had taken over her father's features. It was anger…an anger the likes of which Samira had never seen before.

Samira released her hold on Farid's hand. She wanted to step back, to run from the flames of ire that flashed from her father's eyes. "You are pregnant?" he said.

She nodded, but her father's gaze had already left her and now scorched Farid.

"You, Farid Nasir, have worked for the palace and my family for many years and now I find that you have betrayed my trust, made a mockery of your duty and dishonored not only my daughter, but me as well.''

"Father..."

"Be silent!" Sheik Ahmed's voice thundered at Samira, then turned back to look at Farid once again. Farid remained unmoving beneath the sheik's angry glare. Not a muscle on his face twitched.

"Ahmed," Alima said softly, but the sheik ignored her. He reached up and took hold of the royal patch on Farid's breast pocket and with one vicious yank, ripped the patch completely off.

Samira gasped, tears half-blinding her. Farid remained unmoving, unblinking, not even attempting to defend himself or his honor.

"You have abused your position in the worst possible way. I have lost all trust, all respect for you and for that I banish you from the palace grounds."

"No!" Samira cried out. She shot a pleading look at her mother, who looked as heartbroken, as helpless as Samira felt. "We are married."

"I recognize no such thing. Guards," Sheik Ahmed bellowed as he stepped back from Farid. Instantly two guards appeared in the doorway. "Escort Farid Nasir from the palace grounds immediately."

As Farid left the room with the two guards, Samira turned to her parents. "Father...no...please," she begged. Finding no succor in her father, she turned her attention to her mother. "Mother, please—do something. You have to do something!"

Samira didn't wait to see what her mother might

or might not do. Instead, she whirled around and ran after her husband, who was flanked by the two guards and heading out of the palace.

Ahmed sank back down into his chair behind his desk and buried his face in his hands. Alima walked over to stand beside him and placed a hand on his shoulder.

Theirs had been an arranged marriage, one based on politics, but it had become a marriage of respect and desire and love.

She knew her husband was a man of intense emotions. It was what made him a good ruler but, at times, it could also be his undoing.

"Ahmed…he's her husband," she said softly.

He removed his hands from his face and turned to look at her, his eyes reflecting pain. "I will not recognize their marriage. To do so is to condone what has happened, and it is unforgivable that Farid took advantage of his position with our daughter."

Alima sighed and rubbed a hand across his tense shoulders. "Our daughters have had minds of their own from the moment they were born…because they are princesses, and because they are women. Look at how well Leila and Nadia have chosen."

"That's neither here nor there," he replied tersely, a frown etching deeply into his broad forehead. "Royal bodyguards are held to greater standards than ordinary men and Farid has acted like a man, not a bodyguard. I cannot forgive him for that."

Alima knew her husband well, and she heard the

steely strength in his voice as he spoke these words. She knew that, at least for this moment in time, there was nothing she could do or say that would change his mind.

Perhaps later, after some time had passed and the shock had worn off, he would soften. But for now, emotions were too high to reason with him.

"She's with child, Ahmed," she said softly, unable to stop herself from trying one last time to soften his heart. "Our second grandchild."

"And we will do everything in our power to support Samira and the child she carries," he said. "Tell her that, Alima. Tell her that she and her child will want for nothing, but I will not allow that man back in the palace or on the grounds. He will have no place in my family, in my life or in my heart."

Alima's heart sank, but she kissed her husband on his forehead and hurried out of the room, intent on finding Samira.

She had a feeling her husband hadn't yet realized that in banishing the man Samira loved, he'd banished his daughter as well.

"Farid, wait!"

Farid stopped at the sound of Samira's frantic voice. He and his two guards had just reached the palace's front entrance when she caught up with them.

She ran directly into his arms, burying her tearful face into the front of his jacket. "Oh, Farid. It was far worse than I expected," she cried. "I've never seen him so angry."

She raised her face from his jacket and gazed up at him. "We have to tell him the truth. We have to tell him that you aren't—"

"No." Farid said the word sharply, glancing at the two guards to see how much of the conversation they were taking in. "You made me a promise," he said in an urgent whisper. "And I will not release you from it right now. Perhaps later, when things calm down a bit."

Farid had suspected that Sheik Ahmed's legendary temper would explode and he'd been right. He'd prefer that Sheik Ahmed vent his rage on him, and not on his daughter.

If Sheik Ahmed learned the truth, Farid feared his rage would not only be directed at Desmond Caruso, but at Samira as well. The sheik would not be pleased that Samira had been seduced by a Montebellan right under the sheik's and the king and queen of Montebello's noses. Things were finally going well between the two countries. Peace was more important than Farid's own honor.

Farid was certain that Sheik Ahmed would have preferred that his daughter marry somebody from Tamir—just not her bodyguard.

"What are we going to do?"

He stroked a hand down her shining hair then grabbed her shoulders and held her away from him. "I'm going to my farm, and you're going to stay here.

We'll see what happens when things cool down a bit.''

She looked at him for a long moment, then nodded. He released her, oddly disappointed and unsure why. Without saying another word, he turned and continued out the palace doors.

It was better this way, he told himself as they stepped out into the bright morning sunshine. She belonged here, in the palace with her family. He shouldn't be surprised that she hadn't demanded she go with him to his farm. She would not go against her parents' wishes, and their wish was that she remain here.

Funny, her gentle nature and her revulsion for confrontation of any kind were two of the reasons he loved her. Ultimately, these were the characteristics that would destroy their marriage.

Samira sat in the window seat of her bedroom, nearly lost amid the thick throw pillows beneath her. The view below was of one of the palace's formal gardens and from her vantage point the flowers looked like bursts of color thrown down to the ground by an artistic genius.

She had often sat here as a young girl, wishing on stars in the night skies and dreaming of love. She'd wished for a handsome, strong man who would fill her days and nights with laughter and love, a man who was honorable and would make a wonderful father to the children they would eventually have.

And wasn't that exactly what fate had sent her?

Was Farid not handsome and strong, a man who'd brought her laughter, a man who would make a wonderful father? Had not all of her wishes been granted with him?

And now it seemed that she would be forced to choose between her family and the man that fate had brought into her life.

How she wished her sisters were here for her to talk to. Surely Leila or Nadia would know what she should do. But Leila was in Texas with her husband, Cade, and Nadia was with her husband in Penwyck meeting her in-laws. Samira had never felt so alone.

A knock fell on her door and she was unsurprised when her mother walked in. She rose from the window seat and went directly to her mother's arms.

Alima wrapped her in the kind of hug that only a mother could give, one infused with unconditional love. As the hug continued, tears burned at Samira's eyes. "Oh, mother, things are in such a mess," she said miserably as the hug ended.

Alima led her daughter to the bed and together they sat down, Samira's hands held by her mother's.

"You must talk to Father," Samira said. "Farid is a good man, Mother. He doesn't deserve to be banished from his job, from his life here at the palace."

"Samira, you must understand, you sprang this on us suddenly." Alima frowned and released Samira's hands. "In the months that Farid has been your bodyguard I've never seen a look pass between the two of you, a touch of any kind. This just seems to have happened so fast.'' Alima held Samira's gaze. ''How far along is your pregnancy?''

Samira broke the gaze with her mother. ''A couple of months,'' she replied. She had to hedge a bit, or her mother would wonder how Farid had gotten her pregnant before the two had spent any time together at all.

''Samira, your father is most angry with Farid right now. Your father personally chooses the men to serve as the family bodyguards, and Farid betrayed that trust.''

Samira desperately wanted to tell her mother that Farid hadn't betrayed the trust, that he had been so honorable he'd given his name to her to cover up her dishonor.

But she'd given her promise to Farid, and in truth, she was afraid that at this moment, telling the truth to her father would only make things worse.

''I think perhaps Farid's betrayal cuts deeper than anyone else's because you have always been the most gentle, the most naïve of our children.''

Samira stood and walked back over to the window. ''I'm not feeling very gentle at the moment.'' She sighed tremulously. ''I feel as if my heart is breaking.''

It was at that moment that Samira realized she truly did love Farid. Her love for him filled her up, momentarily making speech impossible.

When had it happened? How was it possible that she had managed to fall in love with the man she had married? The man who had married her not because he loved her, but because he'd believed it was his duty?

She turned back to her mother, her eyes once again awash with tears. "Oh, mother, I don't know what to do."

Alima took her by the shoulders. "Have you seen a doctor since you realized you were pregnant?" Samira shook her head. "Then that's our first order of business. I'll ring Dr. Mallah and we'll go see him immediately."

Once again Samira sank down on the bed. She watched as her mother picked up the phone and made the arrangements with the royal doctor.

Nearly an hour later Samira and her mother left the office of Dr. Mallah. Samira had been given a clean bill of health and Dr. Mallah had assured her that everything seemed to be progressing quite normally with her pregnancy.

The whole time the doctor had talked to her about diet and exercise and what to expect in the coming months, Samira's heart had ached in despair.

"Samira, talk to me," Alima said once they were back in Samira's bedroom. The two women sat together in the window seat, Samira staring out at the gardens below.

She remembered the first time she and Farid had kissed…really kissed. It had been in the gardens of Montebello, when she'd thought the man approaching in the darkness might be Desmond.

Had that been the moment when she'd fallen in love with Farid? When his lips had been so warm against hers? Or had she fallen in love with him as he'd told her silly stories that made her laugh? Or when he'd bared his past to her, talking of the pain of his mother's secret?

"I just don't know what to do. I'm so afraid of making Father more angry," she said softly and turned her gaze to her mother.

"Do you love Farid?" Alima asked.

"With all my heart," Samira answered without hesitation.

"Then you must decide what frightens you more— your father's anger, or being without the man you love." Alima reached out and touched Samira's cheek, her fingers warm against her skin. "Follow your heart, Samira. It will never lead you astray."

With a final pat to Samira's cheek, Alima stood and left the room.

Samira returned her attention out the window. Follow her heart? Could she do that? It would be so easy to remain here in the bosom of her family where she knew she would always be loved.

Follow her heart? *Should* she do that? Even if her heart led to a man who had already told her he would never, *could* never love her in the valentines-and-flowers way she'd once dreamed of being loved?

Chapter 12

There was a sense of welcome in the small farmhouse that hadn't been present in the year since his mother's death. As Farid put away the groceries he'd bought on his way to the farm, he realized that without the anger he'd felt toward his mother, his heart was open to the warmth and love the house possessed.

After putting away the groceries, he drifted from room to room, memories of family pressing thick against his chest. Each room held a special, cherished memory of each of his parents, and he allowed himself to bask in those memories for a little while.

He'd mourned his father deeply at the time of his death so long ago, but the grief he'd felt at the time of his mother's passing had been complicated by anger.

Now he touched one of the needlepoint pillows on

the sofa, his mind filled with a vision of her head bent over the delicate work, a smile lighting her face each time she gazed at him.

A day had not passed that his mother didn't tell him how strong he was, how smart he was, and her words of praise had developed in him a positive self-confidence and esteem that had been unshakable.

He picked up one of the pillows and hugged it, emotion pressing suffocatingly tight in his chest. The house resonated with an emptiness that seemed to feed the sudden despair inside him.

He was alone, and never had he felt his loneliness as deeply as he did at this moment. He'd suffered loneliness in the years following his father's death and eventually he'd become accustomed to the feeling.

But this was different. He set the pillow down and drew a deep breath, fighting against the unsettling feeling that filled him.

It was ridiculous that he should feel so bereft after all this time. His father had been dead for years, his mother for nearly a year. And the biological father that he'd known only briefly had been dead for almost six months. Why was he feeling so empty now?

Samira. Her name exploded in his head, but he shoved thoughts of her aside. He'd known all along that their arrangement in all probability was temporary. He had been prepared for the end of it.

Deciding the best thing to do was to keep busy, he picked up a dust cloth and began to dust the living-room furniture. In the year since his mother's death, he'd only been back to the house a few times and had rarely taken the time to do any housecleaning.

It hadn't really sunk in yet, the fact that he'd lost his position and had been sent away from the palace in shame. If he looked out one of the back windows, he'd be able to see the very top of the palace in the distance.

Surely it was the loss of his job and the disgrace of being commanded off the palace grounds that filled him with such despondency. It had nothing to do with the fact that his marriage to Samira was probably at an end.

He placed his dust cloth on the coffee table and sank down on the sofa, his thoughts chaotic in his head. He'd known someplace deep inside that Sheik Kamal would be angry. He'd also known it was possible he would be the scapegoat for that anger.

However, his job had been to protect Samira and that's what he had done. Although he knew there would be a certain amount of gossip concerning their marriage and her pregnancy, it wouldn't be the same kind of gossip that would have filled the tabloids had she been unmarried and pregnant and the father of her baby was unknown.

A knock on his front door pulled him up off the sofa. Samira? His heart leapt with joy, a joy that was instantly dashed when he opened the door to see a tall, slender old man.

"Izzat!" He greeted the man with a warm hug. "How did you know I was here?" he asked as he gestured the old man across the threshold.

"I was driving by and saw your car, and thought I would stop in and say hello."

"I'm glad you did. It's been far too long. Come, let's go into the kitchen and have something cold to drink."

Izzat Naggar had been an old friend of Farid's father, Hashim. Farid had grown up thinking of Izzat as a favorite uncle. He had visited often when Hashim was alive, though less frequently in the years after Hashim's death.

"You're looking well, Izzat," Farid said as he poured them each a cold drink.

Izzat smiled. "I have the complaints of an old man. My bones ache and my digestion isn't what it once was, but I'm doing all right."

"Your family is well?"

"They are fine."

For a few minutes the two men visited, catching up on what had been happening with each of them. Farid, unsure what the official story might be from the palace, mentioned nothing about his marriage to Samira or the fact that he'd been banished from the palace grounds and fired from his job.

Instead, their talk turned to the old days, when Hashim was alive and Farid was young. Memory recalled memory and the two men laughed, sharing the good days of the past together.

For Farid, the talk was a balm to his wounded spirit, evoking in him a warmth for both his parents and cherished moments he'd thought long forgotten.

It wasn't until Farid sensed that Izzat was getting

ready to leave that he decided to broach the subject of his parentage with him. "Izzat, did you know that Hashim wasn't my biological father?"

The old man leaned back in his chair and stroked his gray beard thoughtfully. "I did. Your father confided in me before you were born."

"I've been trying to figure out why my mother waited so long to tell me the truth," Farid said.

"I can answer that for you. She promised Hashim she wouldn't tell you," Izzat said without hesitation. He stroked his beard once again, his dark gaze warm as it lingered on Farid. "I've never seen a man as besotted with a child as Hashim was with you. The sun rose and set solely for your pleasure as far as he was concerned. He adored you and in his heart you were his and nobody else's."

"Why would he make my mother promise not to tell me the truth?" Farid asked, wanting to understand the forces that had been at work in his parents' lives.

"Hashim knew who your real father was, and I think it threatened him. Hashim loved you so much. He was afraid if you knew the truth, he would lose you. I'm not saying what he did was the right thing to do, but he was only human."

"I loved Hashim. He would have never lost my love." Even now, saying his name evoked a surge of love inside Farid for the man who had been his father for twelve years.

"Ah, Farid, but hindsight is always so much more sharp than foresight. Hashim didn't intend to die when you were young. I'm sure he assumed he would live to see you grown and married with children of your own.''

Farid leaned back in his chair, frowning thoughtfully. ''I wonder why Mother didn't tell me then—when he died—instead of waiting so many more years to finally confess the truth to me.''

''Who knows? Perhaps she was still honoring her promise to Hashim, or she was frightened as well.''

''Frightened of what?''

''She'd already lost her husband, maybe she was afraid that if you knew the truth she would lose you as well.'' Izzat stood. ''Your biological father was a nobleman, a man with money and position. Your mother was a simple woman with simple values. Perhaps she was afraid your head would be turned by the man who fathered you and you would lose sight of all she and Hashim had taught you. And now, my dear Farid, I've got to get to the marketplace.''

Farid walked him out and at the door the two men hugged. ''Stay well, Farid,'' Izzat said. ''Know that you were loved deeply by the two people who raised you.''

Farid nodded and hugged the man one last time, then watched as he headed to his car. He stood in the doorway until the dust from Izzat's car had disappeared, then he closed the door slowly.

Although Farid had believed his discussion with Samira had resolved any resentment he might feel about his mother, had there been any left in his heart, Izzat's words had shoved it out completely.

Farid was left only with love for the parents he

missed and a new emotion that pierced deeply into his heart—the pain of a crazy loneliness he didn't know how to deal with.

He hadn't realized until now how completely Samira had filled up his life, bringing light into the dark corners, pulling laughter from his lips and stoking inside him a passion for life…and for her.

For two weeks they had lived as husband and wife, and he missed her presence here…now.

He hadn't really expected her to defy her father, pack up her bags and move to this small farmhouse. She was a princess, and he was a disgraced bodyguard. He didn't want her here. She deserved better.

As he washed the glasses he and Izzat had used, once again he shoved thoughts of Samira out of his head. Time would tell what became of their so-called marriage.

He'd never believed it was a forever kind of deal. She'd been panicked and heartbroken, and marriage to him had seemed like the answer to her problems, but he'd known deep in his heart all along that she'd simply been afraid of her parents' reaction and had wanted somebody at her side.

He'd done his job and now it was, for all intents and purposes, finished. Now he had to figure out what he was going to do with the rest of his life.

Working for the palace, working in some form of royal security, was all Farid had ever wanted to do. Every choice he'd made in his life, everything he had done had been to achieve that goal. Now it was all gone, and what amazed him was that he'd gladly lose it all again to help Samira.

He had just cleaned up the kitchen when he heard the sound of cars pulling up outside. He hurried to the front door, opened it and stared in astonishment as he saw two palace cars. What now? he thought.

His astonishment increased when the driver of the first car got out and hurried to open the back door and Samira stepped out. At the same time several guards got out of the other car. Samira approached him, a fierce determination on her pretty face.

"Samira, what are you doing here?" he asked. She was still dressed in the silver *jalabiya* she'd had on when they'd confronted her parents. The silver material complemented her skin tones and the darkness of her hair.

She swept past him and into the house, then turned back to him. "Where else would I be but with my husband in his home?" Her gaze went around the room. "And it appears to be a very nice home."

"What about your parents? Do they know you're here?" At that moment the driver appeared in the doorway with two suitcases.

Samira motioned him inside. "Let's just place those in the bedroom. Farid, which room is ours?"

"Second doorway on the right." He gestured down the hallway, shock still rippling through him.

"What a lovely room," she said a moment later as she and the driver returned from the bedroom. "I notice it will get the sun in the mornings. That will be nice."

The driver left, and as Farid closed the front door after him, he noticed that two guards were now stationed at the entrance of his driveway. He suspected that two more were probably at the back of his house.

He turned back to Samira, who had sat on the sofa and gazed at him expectantly. "Would you like to tell me what's going on?"

"There's nothing going on. I'm where I belong—with my husband." She raised her chin and held his gaze intently.

Farid sat next to her, noting the lines of tension around her eyes…eyes that showed the telltale signs of recent tears. "And your father has given his blessing to you being here?"

She quickly looked down at her hands in her lap. "Not exactly. Right after you left, my mother insisted I see the physician and get a complete check-up."

"And everything is all right?" he asked urgently.

"Oh, yes." She raised her gaze to meet his and smiled reassuringly. "He informs me that I'm in perfect health and everything is fine with the pregnancy." A wave of relief swept through Farid.

"After I had my check-up, I had a discussion with my mother."

"You did not tell her the truth, I hope."

Samira shook her head, her dark hair swirling around her shoulders. "No, I kept my promise to you and didn't tell her the truth. But after talking to her, I realized I needed to speak with my father once again, so I went back to his office to talk to him."

She laced, then unlaced her hands in her lap, looking down once again. "He was still very angry...more angry than I've ever seen him in my life. I demanded that he give you back your job and allow you back into the palace."

Again astonishment swept through him. "You demanded?"

A small smile curved one corner of her mouth. "Yes. I'm not sure who was more surprised, my father or me. Needless to say, he only got angrier. I told him that if he didn't allow you at the palace, then I would have to leave, and he forbade me to leave."

"Then you shouldn't be here." Farid stood. "You need to go back." The last thing Farid wanted was to be the cause of a permanent break between daughter and father.

"I will not go back. My place is here with you." Once again she raised her chin and eyed him with a steely resolve he'd never seen before.

"You are Princess Samira Kamal and you belong at the palace," he exclaimed.

"I am Samira Nasir and I belong wherever you are," she countered.

He stood, needing some distance from her. He needed to stand where he couldn't smell her lovely, fragrant scent, walk far enough away that he couldn't feel the sweet heat radiating from her body.

"I am an outcast, Samira. I have been banished from the palace grounds. I have lost my job."

"Then you will find a new job," she said briskly. She stood. "And now, why don't you show me our home."

This wasn't right, he thought as he led her into the large, airy kitchen with the modern conveniences he had installed over the years.

"How nice," she exclaimed. "And decorated in yellow." She smiled at him. "Did you know that yellow is my favorite color?"

"No, I didn't know that," he said absently. He was still shocked by her appearance here and the news that she'd fought with her father on his behalf.

"And what's your favorite color, Farid?" she asked.

Whatever color you're wearing, he thought, but he didn't speak the words aloud. "We have more important things to discuss than favorite colors."

"You're right," she agreed. "Like how many bedrooms there are."

He sighed in frustration and followed behind her as she swept out of the kitchen and down the hallway, stopping at the first bedroom on the left and stepping inside.

Her gaze swept around the small room, lingering on the small bed with its navy spread, the collection of children's books on the shelf and the drawings that decorated the walls.

"This was your room?" she asked, standing before the drawings, a smile curving her lips. He nodded. "And this is your artwork?" The pictures were of different angles of the palace.

"Yeah. The year before Hashim died, he bought me a set of drawing pencils." He stuffed his hands in his pockets and leaned against the door jamb. "I tried drawing people, but had no talent for that. It was Hashim's idea that I try to draw buildings.''

''They're very good,'' she said.

He grinned. ''Yeah, they aren't bad for an eleven-year-old.'' His smile faded and he pulled his hands from his pockets. ''Samira—''

''There's a third bedroom, isn't there?'' She swept past him back into the hallway. She disappeared into the smaller third bedroom and again Farid watched her from the doorway as she looked around the room that had been his mother's sewing room.

''This will make a perfect nursery,'' she exclaimed. ''We won't even have to repaint, this peach color is lovely.''

For just a moment Farid's head was filled with a vision…a crib by the window, a rocking chair nearby. The room would smell of baby powder and Samira's sweet scent. He could see her sitting in the rocking chair, singing softly as she soothed their baby to sleep.

He shook his head to dispel the image, knowing it was one that would never come true. He couldn't give her what she wanted, what she needed for a happily ever after, and he knew she wasn't here because she loved him desperately.

She was here because she felt grateful to him, because she didn't know what else to do. He needed to send her home before the chasm between her and her parents got too wide to breach.

''Samira, come back to the living room. We need to talk.''

Her gaze held his for a long moment. "I don't think I want to," she replied.

What Farid wanted to do was to wrap her in his arms, pull her close against his chest where he could feel her heart beating against his own.

What he wanted to do was to kiss her trembling mouth until she gasped with pleasure, but doing those things would solve nothing.

Instead he held out a hand to her and together they walked from the small spare room back into the living room. As they passed the front window a shaft of sunlight caught the gold of the ring on her finger and it seemed to wink at him, mocking him.

A princess deserved better than a plain gold band. This princess deserved better than a man who'd been dishonored and banished and had no idea what his own personal future might hold.

It was time to send her back home where she belonged.

He led her to the sofa and they sat side by side. "Don't send me away, Farid," she said, as if she'd read his thoughts and was attempting to preempt him. Her eyes sparkled with the reflection of her silver dress. "I won't leave. I belong here…with you."

"Samira, you belong in the palace, with your family who loves you," he replied, trying not to notice the hurt that resided in her almond eyes.

Still, he continued, wanting her to understand all that she was giving up to be here with him now. "Samira, you will want your parents and your siblings surrounding you, especially as your pregnancy progresses.''

"I will want my husband with me," she countered.

Before he could reply there was a brisk knock on the front door.

Frowning, Farid got up from the sofa and went to the front door. He was surprised to see two armed palace guards. Farid recognized them both, although he knew neither very well.

"Yes?" He looked at them expectantly.

"Farid Nasir, we are to escort you back to the palace," the eldest guard said.

Samira joined Farid at the door and grabbed his arm, a beatific smile lighting her face. "Farid, perhaps Father has changed his mind!"

Moments later Samira sat next to him in the back of the official car and squeezed his hand tightly. "I knew Father's anger couldn't last forever," she said. "I'm sure he has called you back to make things right."

"Samira, I wouldn't be too quick to get my hopes up if I were you," he warned.

A bad feeling filled him as he stared out the window at the approaching palace gates. His instincts were screaming that something was wrong—something was *terribly* wrong.

If Sheik Ahmed had changed his mind about Farid's banishment, he wouldn't have sent armed guards to escort him back to the palace.

Chapter 13

Samira sat next to Farid in the back of the car, her heart filled with a new joy. Her father was going to relent. She was sure of it. He would relent and apologize to Farid and everything would be wonderful.

She still couldn't believe that she'd stood up to her father. For the first time in her life she'd met him shout for shout, demanding he remove his banishment of Farid. The sheik had not relented, and for the first time in her life, neither had Samira.

"You must decide what frightens you more...your father's anger, or being without the man you love." Alima's words had played and replayed in Samira's head and after surprisingly little thought, she'd known which frightened her more.

Breaking ties with her father would be painful, but living without Farid was impossible to fathom. She drew a deep breath, certain that her father had had a change of heart and now intended to welcome Farid into the family.

She gazed at Farid now, fighting the impulse to reach out and take his hand. She wanted to tell him how much she loved him. Her love for him ached inside her with the need to be verbalized, but now was not the place or the time.

She wasn't sure there would ever be a time or a place for her to speak to him of how deeply, how profoundly she'd come to love him.

Love had never been part of their marriage arrangement, although certainly passion had sprung to life between them. Was passion enough to keep them together for a lifetime?

She frowned and shoved the question out of her head. Looking at him again, she felt the distance that radiated from him, saw the frown that cut deeply across his brow.

He'd never said he loved her. He'd never even intimated such a thing. Instead of looking happy that her father might have relented about his banishment, he looked tense and worried.

Maybe he didn't want her father to relent. Maybe it had been his intention all along to get her back home, back in the loving arms of her family, then separate from her.

As they turned into the palace gates, she felt an overwhelming sense of despair. Had her fight with her father been for nothing? For the first time in her entire life she'd stood up and fought for what she wanted, but had she fought for something that ultimately she could never have?

Duty. That's why he had married her. Was it fair for her to keep him bound to her when he didn't love her? He was an honorable man who would, in all probability, stand by his duty and the vows they had taken as long as she wanted. Was her love for him enough to make her happy?

And what of his happiness?

At the moment, there was no more thought of anything but the immediate future. The car pulled up in front of the palace and Samira and Farid were escorted inside.

To her surprise, they were not taken into her father's private office where they had spoken to him that morning, but rather into the grand chamber—the room used for official business and to greet visiting dignitaries.

For the first time since the two guards had appeared at Farid's house, a sense of disquiet swept through Samira. Perhaps her father had not relented after all.

The guards took positions in the back of the room, leaving Samira and Farid alone before the dais and the throne from which Sheik Ahmed Kamal ruled his country.

"I can't imagine what's going on," she whispered to Farid, who stood at attention as if prepared to face a firing squad. "I don't understand why we were brought in here," she said, her anxiety growing by the minute.

At that moment her father entered the room. When

they had met with him earlier he had been dressed casually, but now he was dressed formally, in the splendor of Tamir tradition.

Clad in a deep-purple jacket and a white *shalwar,* he carried himself with a dignity and presence that commanded respect.

On his head he wore a matching dark-purple turban embedded with pearls, rubies and emeralds, completing the imperial aura.

Samira's stomach tied itself in knots as he took his seat on the throne, his gaze meeting neither hers nor Farid's. Alima entered next and sat in the smaller chair next to his, her eyes downcast above the traditional veil that covered the lower portion of her face.

Samira's uneasiness reached a fever pitch inside her. What was going on? This was far too formal and her parents looked far too solemn for this to be a family forgiveness kind of session.

"Guards," Sheik Ahmed bellowed. "Please bring in our visitors."

Visitors?

Samira turned around to see two Montebellan officials between the two Tamiri guards. What on earth was going on? The tension in the room was positively air-stealing.

"Father?" Samira looked at Sheik Ahmed worriedly.

"These men are here to speak with Farid Nasir. Farid, this is Inspector Faud and Inspector Najib from Montebellan Royal Security," Sheik Ahmed said.

"Farid Nasir?" The shorter of the two spoke. "I'm

Inspector Faud.'' He was a swarthy-looking man with little eyes and instantly Samira didn't like him.

"Yes?'' He eyed the two men. "What can I do for you?''

"We're here to ask you some questions about Desmond Caruso,'' Inspector Faud explained.

Desmond? Samira's thoughts whirled. Was it possible that Desmond was pressing charges against Farid for the incident last night in the restaurant?

If this was the case, Samira desperately hoped the whole thing didn't spin out of control. The peace between Tamir and Montebello was new, although made solid by the marriage of her brother Rashid to the Montebellan princess, Julia. Their young son, Omar, was a physical embodiment of the countries' new friendly relationship. If King Marcus got angry over the abuse of his nephew by a Tamiri bodyguard, then the peace could become strained, and who knew what would happen between the two small kingdoms?

"What about him?'' Farid replied, his voice thick with his obvious dislike of Caruso.

The two inspectors exchanged glances with each other.

"What exactly is this all about?'' Samira asked. She focused her question to the taller of the two, Inspector Najib.

"We understand that you and Desmond had an altercation in the Glass Swan Restaurant yesterday evening,'' Inspector Faud said, his beady eyes narrowed.

It seemed impossible that it had only been yesterday that she and Farid had enjoyed a nice dinner—a dinner that had been ruined by the horrible words Desmond had spoken to her and the resulting fracas between him and Farid.

"We did," Farid answered. "He insulted the princess and I felt he needed to be taught some manners." He looked from one to the other of the inspectors. "Has Caruso decided to press charges? Is that what this is all about?"

"I'm afraid Caruso won't be pressing much of anything. He was found dead this morning in his guest house," Inspector Najib exclaimed.

"Dead?" Samira gasped as her knees threatened to buckle beneath her. Farid grabbed her arm and pulled her against him to steady her.

Desmond dead? Her mind struggled to comprehend what the inspector had just said. Was it possible Farid had somehow hurt him, resulting in an accidental death?

"He's dead?" Farid's shock was obvious as he stared at the two men before him.

Dead? Desmond was dead? She wrapped her arms around her stomach as if to shield the baby she carried from the news. Samira hadn't wanted Desmond to be a part of her child's life, and now he never would be.

However, as much as she'd hated the way Desmond had betrayed her, as much as she hated the way he had talked to her in the restaurant, she certainly had never wished him dead.

She shot a frightened look at Farid. A pulse ticked at his jaw, a telling sign of nervous tension.

"What happened to him?" Farid asked.

"We were hoping you could tell us that. I'm afraid you will have to return to Montebello with us, Mr. Nasir," Inspector Faud said, his gaze cold as it lingered on Farid. "We have a lot of questions for you concerning the murder of Desmond Caruso."

"Murder?" Farid's body stiffened.

"Murder?" Samira gasped again and leaned weakly against her husband, positively stunned by the news.

"Caruso was murdered in cold blood in his guest house. A maid found him early this morning in his bedroom," Faud explained.

"How...what killed him?" It was obvious Farid was as stunned by the news as Samira. The pulse in his jaw worked frantically and his hands were clenched into fists at his sides.

"He was hit in the back of the head by some instrument with a tremendous amount of force. He died instantly," Faud explained as he pulled a set of handcuffs from his pocket.

"Wait!" Samira said, feeling as if the whole world had gone crazy. "It's impossible. Farid didn't murder Desmond...he couldn't have." Samira stepped forward in an effort to make the two officials understand. "I know Farid, and he is not a murderer," she said fervently. "Besides, he was with me all night."

Farid grabbed her arm and pulled her back, stepping in front of her as if to shield her from the gazes of the two men.

"You'll have a chance to explain your alibi or whatever when we return to Tamir. At the moment we have eyewitnesses of you threatening to kill Caruso. More than a dozen people in the restaurant heard you threaten him.''

Farid nodded. ''That's true. I did threaten him, but I didn't murder him.''

Inspector Faud smiled thinly. ''We can't just take your word for that. In any case, the threats at the restaurant are only one incident pointing to your explosive temper that has been brought to our attention. Somebody else has come forward with a similar complaint.''

''This is ridiculous. Farid doesn't have an explosive temper.'' Samira's anger was growing along with her fear.

''A reporter has come forward to say that you got quite violent with him.''

Tension rolled from Farid. ''He was attempting to take pictures of the princess—pictures she didn't want taken. I merely took his camera from him and exposed the film.''

Inspector Najib took a step toward Farid and Samira. ''I'm afraid you must come with us, Mr. Nasir. We will continue our interrogation in Montebello.''

''Father! Do something,'' Samira cried and for the first time in her life her father seemed utterly helpless. She left Farid's side, ran to her father and sank down at his knees. ''I beg of you, Father. Please don't let them take him. He did nothing. He's innocent!''

''Samira, I cannot stop an official investigation, especially an investigation into the murder of King Marcus's nephew,'' he said, pain obvious in his dark eyes.

With tears half-blinding her, she got up and ran back to Farid's side, a deep, wrenching sob choking from her as Inspector Faud pulled Farid's hands behind his back and handcuffed him.

Samira clung to Farid, as if by sheer willpower alone she could keep him by her side. Had she stood up to her father, only now to have Farid taken away on a murder charge?

"Samira," Farid said, wishing his hands were free so he could hold her in his arms, tell her that somehow, someway, everything would be all right. "Don't let me leave here with the sounds of your crying the last thing I hear. Besides, all those tears can't be good for our baby."

She straightened and swiped at the tears in her eyes, showing him a strength he wouldn't have guessed she possessed. "This is a terrible miscarriage of justice," she said. "I'm telling you he was with me all night long."

"We have a job to do, Princess," Inspector Najib said, his voice soft, yet respectful. "His alibi will be checked out thoroughly."

Farid felt as if he'd been plunged into a nightmare and no matter how hard he tried, he couldn't wake up. The handcuffs bit into his wrists and his head swam with questions.

Who could have killed Desmond Caruso? The man was slimy enough, there must be a hundred people who would have loved to see him dead.

But, more important, how in the hell was Farid

going to prove himself innocent? Although Samira would swear that he had been with her, how seriously would they take her alibi when they realized she was his wife?

He had to admit, the scene in the restaurant last night certainly didn't help his case for innocence.

As Inspector Faud grabbed his hands to lead him from the grand chamber, Farid was grateful to see Alima leave her seat and hurry to Samira's side.

They had walked only a couple of steps when Farid thought of something. He stopped in his tracks. "When did this happen? Has a medical examiner determined the time of Desmond's death?" Farid looked from Inspector Faud to Inspector Najib.

The two men exchanged glances once again, then Faud shrugged. "The medical examiner has determined the time of death to be between the hours of ten p.m. and two a.m."

"Then it's impossible to tie me to the murder," Farid replied, relief coursing through him. "Not only because I'm innocent, but also because Samira and I were on the plane to return here to Tamir before ten last night."

"That's right," Samira exclaimed. "He couldn't have murdered Desmond and been on the plane at the same time."

"We got in here just after midnight," Farid continued. "You can check the flight records, talk to the pilot. Better yet, talk to the driver of the car who took us to the airport in Montebello. It was one of your own palace cars that took us to the airport."

Once again the two inspectors exchanged glances with one another. "Is there a telephone we could use?" Inspector Faud asked.

"I'll show you where you can make your calls in private," Alima replied and led the two men out of the office.

There followed an uncomfortable silence as Farid, Samira and Sheik Kamal awaited the return of the Montebellan officials.

Samira moved once again to stand at his side and Farid breathed deeply of her scent, wondering, if they took him to Montebello to face murder charges, when he would ever see her, smell her, touch her again.

Samira's father stared at some point above his head, his reproach unspoken, but thick and oppressive. No matter what came from this particular trauma, Farid was certain that the sheik had not softened where he was concerned.

As the moments ticked by, Farid's tension rose. Would they be able to contact the driver who had taken them to the airstrip last night? Would they be able to contact the proper authorities at the airport to confirm the time of their flight?

Samira leaned against him, as if attempting to offer him strength and reassure him. When he looked down at her and into her eyes, he saw her fear...fear for him.

At that moment Alima returned with the two investigators. "It would seem that your alibi for the time of the murder stands up," Najib said.

Relief flooded through Farid.

"I told you he didn't have anything to do with it," Samira said. "Now, I demand that you take those handcuffs off him."

Farid looked at her in surprise. It would appear his gentle, nonconfrontational wife had grown a dainty pair of claws.

Najib gave a curt bow, then walked behind Farid to unfasten the handcuffs. "We apologize for any inconvenience we have caused you, but it's our job to check out all leads."

"He had a woman friend," Samira said suddenly. "Desmond was with her last night in the restaurant. You might want to ask her some questions."

"Do you know who she is? What her name is?" Faud asked.

Samira shook her head with obvious disappointment. "No. I'm sorry, I don't know."

"Can you tell us what she looked like?"

Samira frowned thoughtfully. "I only saw her from the back…she had shoulder-length blond hair and she was tall, and slender. That's all I can tell you. I think they were lovers," she said, her cheeks flushing a pretty pink.

"We'll check it out. And now, we must return immediately to Montebello," Faud said. The two men bowed to the sheik, then left the room.

"Father—" Samira began.

Sheik Ahmed raised a hand. "Nothing has changed, Samira. My banishment of Farid still stands."

Samira looked up at Farid, then drew a deep breath.

''Father, you don't know the whole truth and now it's time the whole truth is told.''

''Samira,'' Farid protested.

Again she looked at her husband. ''I know I promised you, Farid. But now the promise has become too painful to keep. It's time to tell the truth. The whole truth.''

Chapter 14

Samira drew a deep breath to steady herself, then faced her parents once again. She consciously kept her gaze away from Farid, knowing she was about to break her promise to him.

"Samira, what's going on?" Alima asked, her plump face radiating worry. "What truth?"

Sheik Ahmed stood once again, as if preparing himself for another blow from his daughter. "Speak what's on your mind, Samira."

"Samira, you don't have to do this," Farid said, the tension in his voice letting her know he wasn't happy that she was about to break her promise to him.

"You're right," she replied. "I don't have to do this. I could just keep my mouth shut and allow my father to punish you for sins you didn't commit." She shot a quick glance to Farid, whose eyes were as dark as she'd ever seen them. "It's time, Farid. I have to do this now."

She looked back at her parents. "It began almost four months ago at Hassan's wedding," she began. She reached for Farid's hand, hoping he would forgive her for breaking her promise to him.

"What began four months ago?" Sheik Ahmed's eyes were dark, turbulent storm clouds as he gazed at his daughter.

"My affair with the man who is the father of my child. My affair with Desmond Caruso."

"What?" Sheik Ahmed stared at her as if she'd just announced that she was pregnant with twin camels. He sank back into his chair, his gaze not leaving Samira. "You'd better explain yourself, Samira, and you'd better do it quickly. This morning is already wearing on me."

Alima moved to stand next to her husband, her face reflecting her utter surprise at Samira's confession.

"You may remember Desmond stayed as a guest here for a week after the wedding. He was so smooth...so charming." She looked down, unable to gaze at her parents while she told them of her affair. "He told me he loved me and I believed him. He told me we would be married, and I believed every one of his lies."

She was grateful to feel Farid's fingers gently squeezing hers, as if to give her the strength to continue what she had begun. "Three weeks ago I took a pregnancy test and it came back positive. I didn't go to Montebello to visit with Princess Anna. I went to tell Desmond the news and to plan our future together.''

"Desmond was not pleased?" Alima guessed, her features filled with compassion for her daughter.

Samira sighed. "I never got an opportunity to tell him. I went to his guest house and saw him through the window with another woman.''

"If the man wasn't dead already, I would make him wish for death," Sheik Ahmed said harshly.

"Ahmed," Alima said softly, as if cautioning her husband of speaking ill of the dead. "Go on, Samira.''

"I was upset. I was frightened of what you both would think of me, scared to return here pregnant and alone. It was then that Farid offered to marry me—to give my baby his name, and to shield me from your anger. He made it so I wouldn't have to confess to my stupidity where Desmond was concerned. The peace between our kingdoms would not be threatened.''

She looked at Farid, wondering if he could see the love for him that filled her up. She looked back at her father. "Farid did not abuse his position as my bodyguard. Nor did he dishonor you or me. He has done nothing but protect me. He did what he believed was his duty in marrying me.''

Sheik Ahmed raked a hand across his lower jaw, obviously assessing everything that Samira had just told him. "You should have told me all these things this morning.''

"I know," she agreed. She straightened her shoulders and raised her chin. "I am ashamed to admit that I was afraid to tell the truth."

"And I had made her promise not to tell you all this until we both agreed the time was right," Farid said.

"Ahmed, you have something to say to Farid," Alima said pointedly.

"Yes, yes." He stood. "I owe you an apology, Farid."

"No apology is necessary," Farid replied. "You reacted to what you knew and you didn't know the whole truth. I would do whatever it takes to protect your family. It's in my blood to do so."

Sheik Ahmed gazed at him for a long moment. "It is in your blood to do so," he repeated. "An interesting choice of words. A dear, trusted friend of mine many times used that same phrase. His name was Haroun Dharr. Did you know him?"

Samira looked at Farid curiously. Haroun Dharr had been a good friend of her father's. Surely Farid didn't know the nobleman?

Farid hesitated, then nodded. "Haroun Dharr was my father."

"Why did I not know of this?" Sheik Ahmed asked as Samira looked at Farid in surprise.

"I only learned that he was my father a year ago, just before my mother passed away," Farid explained.

"Then why did Haroun not tell me about you? He knew you worked for the palace."

"He didn't know of my existence until a year ago, and then I specifically asked him not to tell you. I wanted my merits to be based on performance, not on my blood ties to a man who was your friend,'' Farid said.

Pride swept through Samira. How she loved this strong, proud man who was her husband. It didn't surprise her that he'd wanted no special treatment due to her father's friendship with his father.

Sheik Ahmed sat once again. "And he was a dear friend. His passing has left a hole in my life."

"And in mine," Farid replied. "He told me how you saved his life when you were both young soldiers, and that he had vowed to you his loyalty and service for the rest of his life. He asked me to continue to carry out that vow and so I have pledged my life to you as my father did before me."

"It is enough that you have bound yourself to my wayward daughter," Sheik Ahmed exclaimed, but his gaze was filled with abiding affection as it lingered on Samira. "I will assign a new bodyguard, for it is not right for your husband to fulfill that position."

Happiness swelled inside her as she realized her father had just accepted the man she loved as her husband. There would be no more talk of banishment or dishonor.

He looked at Farid once again. "We will talk later about a new position for you besides the one you now serve as my son-in-law. I welcome you into the family, Farid Nasir. My daughter has made a good choice for a husband. We will talk more soon, once I have finished the business I have to attend to."

Samira and Farid left the grand chamber. The moment they were out in the hallway, Samira took his hand in hers.

"Would you walk with me in the garden?" she asked. The happiness she'd felt only moments before had been fleeting, for now other thoughts were intruding into her head. Painful thoughts that she needed to sort out.

"Of course," he agreed.

She gestured toward a nearby doorway that led out into a small garden. They stepped out of the doors and into the morning sunshine. The air was rife with floral scents and the murmur of a water fountain broke the silence.

Instantly Samira was reminded of the garden in Montebello where she and Farid had first shared a real, heart-stopping kiss. "You're right," she said. "The gardens here in Tamir are much prettier than the ones in Montebello."

He smiled, but the smile didn't quite reach his eyes and she knew he was probably thinking about how close he'd come to being arrested and taken back to Montebello. "I'm just glad I'm not on my way to Montebello now."

She returned his smile. "Me, too."

They walked a few moments in silence, then she drew him toward a concrete bench near the fountain. "Let's sit for a moment."

"All right," he agreed.

They sat side by side on the bench and Samira fought the impulse to lean against him. "This has been the craziest day of my life," she finally said.

"I think we can agree on that." He stretched his legs out before him and she saw the tension lines that had tightened his features slowly fade away.

"I can't believe the news about Desmond," she said.

"Nor can I," he agreed. "But if he treated other people as he treated you, then who knows who might have wanted him dead."

She sighed. "I didn't want Desmond to be a part of my baby's life, but this isn't the way I wanted to get my wish."

"I know." He reached for her hand as if to offer her some comfort.

Again love for him swelled up inside her, a love that was complicated by other emotions as well. She tried to keep her thoughts focused on their conversation. "I wonder if his murder had anything to do with the woman he was seeing." She frowned thoughtfully. "I wish I could have given the inspectors more information about her."

"Put it out of your mind, Samira. You did the best you could. Leave the murder investigation to the authorities."

"Thank goodness you didn't have to return to Montebello and try to prove your innocence there." This time she gave his hand a small squeeze.

He nodded. "I never again in my life want to feel the bite of handcuffs around my wrists."

"I hope you aren't angry with me," she said.

He looked at her in obvious surprise. "Why would I be angry with you?"

"For breaking my promise."

"When a promise to keep a secret causes pain, then it is time to break the promise." He released her hand and instead raked it through his hair, a frown appearing in his forehead.

"Before you got to the farmhouse today an old friend of the family stopped by to see me. I asked him why my mother had never told me about my real father and he told me my mother had promised Hashim not to tell me."

Samira watched the play of emotions that swept across his face as he spoke of his past. Again her love for him welled up inside her.

"Would my life have been different had my mother broken that promise upon Hashim's death? In truth I don't know, but somehow there is nothing but acceptance in my heart where my mother and her decisions are concerned." The smile he gave her warmed her. "You were right. My mother's only motivation was love."

"I'm glad, Farid, glad you have found peace."

He looked at her, a hint of amusement in his eyes. "You were very brave in there, to tell your father the truth and risk having his wrath directed at you. It would seem my gentle, sweet-natured wife has gained some strength."

"Only when it comes to things and people I desperately care about," she replied. A wave of despair swept through her as she realized what she was about to do—what she had to do.

"Telling my father was the right thing to do." She

looked down at her hands in her lap, her heart aching with the words she knew she was about to speak. "Why did you make me promise not to tell my father the truth, when the truth would clear your name and honor in my father's eyes?" she asked.

"I know your father's reputation for having a rather volatile temper. I knew that it would be easier on you if his ire was directed at me. And I wished to protect the newfound peace between Tamir and Montebello."

Samira nodded, then raised her face to the sun, wishing the warmth would banish the chill that filled her up. He'd been willing to sacrifice his honor, his reputation, his livelihood to protect her and his country.

Again her tremendous love for him filled every pore of her body. He would continue to sacrifice himself for her. For as long as she wanted him as her husband, she knew he would remain by her side.

But was it right for her to keep him by her side? Was it right to bind him to her with his sense of duty? Was it right for her to think only of her happiness and not of his? Would he not eventually grow to resent her?

"What's wrong, Samira?"

She looked at him once again, vaguely surprised that he could read her so well. "Farid, I know that you married me because you felt it was your duty. I know that you were trying to protect me, but now there is nothing to protect me from."

She drew a deep breath, willing away the tears that

burned hot at her eyes. "I just want you to know, Farid, that I appreciate everything you have done for me and my baby. I will forever be grateful to you. You are a wonderful man and I would love to spend the rest of my life with you, but if you wish, I will release you from our marriage."

Her words shocked him. The last thing he'd expected from her was the offer of his freedom from their marriage. His heart suddenly pounded in a rhythm that sent dread coursing through him.

"Is that what you wish?" he asked, the words coming from him with difficulty.

She didn't reply, nor did she look at him. Her gaze remained focused on her hands in her lap, making it impossible for him to see her eyes.

"Samira...is that what you wish? An end to our marriage?" He reached out and took her chin in his hand and tilted her head up so she had to look at him. Her eyes were awash with tears.

"No," she said, the word a mere whisper. "But I love you too much to hold on to you if you don't want to be with me."

"You love me?"

She nodded, looking as if the whole thing made her miserable. "It was my love for you that made me brave enough to face my father, Farid. I love you in a way I'd only dreamed of loving before."

Farid had believed that she couldn't have said anything more that would surprise him. He'd been wrong. She loved him. He couldn't doubt the love that shone from her eyes, couldn't forget how strong she had been on his behalf.

For the first time, Farid had to examine his feelings where she was concerned. He thought of those moments alone in his house when his heart had been burdened by bereavement...not for his parents, but rather for the marriage he feared would end.

Her words of love not only surprised him, but filled him up with warmth and made him realize what was in his own heart. Love.

He took her hands in his and gazed into her sweet brown eyes. "You asked me once if I'd ever been in love and I told you that I didn't believe in the valentine-and-flowers kind of love you were talking about. How could I believe in something I'd never experienced before?"

She nodded and started to pull her hands from his, but he held tight, refusing to relinquish his hold. "When your father first assigned me to be your personal bodyguard, I was glad he'd assigned me to you. You were gentle and kind and never gave anyone any problems, and I thought that's why I was happy about the assignment, because you'd be easy."

A small burst of laughter escaped her. "Little did you know," she said dryly.

He squeezed her hands. "Now, looking back, I realize I was glad I was assigned to you because I liked your smile and the sound of your laughter. Because I had watched you from the time I first began working at the palace, when I was nineteen and you were only sixteen. I was glad that I was assigned to you because

I wanted to be around you and spend time in your presence.''

Her tears had dried and there was a look of wonder in her beautiful eyes, and in that wonder the full force of Farid's feelings for her opened up completely in his heart.

''When I got to my house today, I was fairly certain that it was the beginning of the end of our marriage. I found myself wondering how my life was going to be without the sound of your laughter in it, how I was going to survive the nights without you in my arms.''

''Farid?'' There was a question in her voice.

''Samira, somehow in the last two weeks, you've taken my heart and turned it into a valentine. You've taken my life and transformed it into a garden of flowers. You've made me believe in love, because I am helplessly, hopelessly in love with you.''

He stood and pulled her up into his arms, loving the way she fit so neatly against him. As if they were two halves and were only truly complete when together.

''I love you, Samira, and I want our marriage to last through eternity. I want to be the father to the child you carry and father a dozen more with you.''

''Oh, Farid. I love you so…''

He cut off anything else she might be going to say by claiming her lips with his, the kiss filled with all the passion, all the tenderness and all the love he possessed inside him.

He tasted the same depth of emotions in her lips and he reveled in them. When the kiss finally ended her eyes shone bright and he knew this was the woman he wanted to wake up with every morning, the woman he wanted in his arms each night when he fell asleep.

He smiled at her. "I love you, Samira Nasir. You're my princess…my love…my life."

"And I love you, Farid Nasir," the warmth of her eyes spoke the words as eloquently as her lips. "You are my love and my life."

Once again they shared a kiss that spoke not only of devotion and commitment, but of a future filled with joy and happiness, and the valentines-and-flowers kind of love.

* * * * *

Chapter 1

Ryan McDonough gave the woman the once-over, noting the thinly concealed frustration in her sin-dark eyes and her subtly defensive stance. "I'm sorry for your loss, Ms. Caruso," he said automatically, words repeated countless times to families of countless victims. "I understand your offer to help, but what you want is not possible."

He was sorry to see anyone grieve. God knows he knew what it was like. Grief in this instance must already have passed beyond tears to the second phase. Anger. She was gritting her teeth.

However, the Caruso woman inclined her head and said, "Thank you for your condolences, but I must insist." Very proper. But still not acceptable.

Ryan kept a cool head. It usually gave him the advantage.

"We have nothing to discuss, ma'am," he told her calmly. "The king will have my preliminary report on your brother's death first thing in the morning and any further information as soon as I discover it. His Majesty's advisors will keep you up to date." He got up and went to open the door to show her out.

She sighed, walked around his desk and sat down in his chair, big as you please. *His* chair. Propping her elbows on the arms of it, she steepled her fingers under her chin. She had great hands. Long, supple fingers tipped with fairly short nails painted wine-red to match her lips. He tried not to look at the lips, but they kept drawing his attention even when she wasn't speaking.

Ryan shook off his fascination, disgruntled with himself for noticing her looks and with her for provoking him to notice.

"I didn't come halfway around the world to sit somewhere and wait," she declared, her voice clipped and precise, totally devoid of an accent. "My brother's been killed and I'm sticking to you like Super Glue until we find out who did it. Get used to it."

Ryan fought hard for patience. She might be rude, but he hated to be sharp with her. That wasn't his way, especially when she was probably just upset about her half brother's violent death.

Probably being the key word here. Now that he looked at her more objectively, she didn't appear to be all that grief-stricken. And she was dangerously close to pushing the wrong button on his control panel, barging in here demanding to be part of the case.

He sat on the corner of his desk, assuming a relaxed pose, wishing he felt relaxed. "Look, Ms. Caruso—"

"Nina," she said curtly. "We might as well get acquainted since we'll be spending a great deal of time together. Why don't you begin by listing what you've found out so far. You've had two full days and part of this one." She paused for a second, then added, "Mac."

Ryan bit his tongue and unclenched his fist, deliberately projecting benevolence and goodwill. She didn't react as expected to outright dismissal. He'd try manners. Not usually his *last* resort and shouldn't be now, but they had gotten off on the wrong foot the minute she'd walked in.

Empathize first, he thought. "Of course you want to know what's going on and I understand that completely. You may read copies of the reports tomorrow if His Majesty sees fit to share them with you. Until then, I must ask you to excuse me so that I can continue to do my job." There. Polite and to the point. *Get lost, Cookie.*

"King Marcus assured me you would welcome my help," she said.

"I regret to say he was wrong."

The door opened. Duke Lorenzo Sebastiani, head of Montebello's Royal Intelligence, entered without preamble. "Good morning," he said formally. Nina rose from the chair.

Ryan eyed him with suspicion. "In case you two

haven't met, Nina Caruso, this is His Grace, Duke Lorenzo Sebastiani.''

Lorenzo reached for her hand and bowed over it. ''I regret we must meet for the first time in such terrible circumstances. I share in your grief.''

''Thank you, Your Grace,'' she mumbled, obviously a little taken aback and unsure what else she should say.

She made a perfect curtsy, however.

Ryan managed a nod, his version of a bow, in Lorenzo's direction.

''I am so sorry to have missed your arrival at the palace,'' Lorenzo said graciously. ''The king has explained your mission to me.''

He then addressed Ryan. ''Nina's participation in the investigation is not simply a request. It is her right as a sister, I believe.''

''I see,'' Ryan said, tasting dry defeat. ''Her right? Some new custom I'm not aware of?''

''Precisely,'' Lorenzo affirmed. ''There will be no problem accommodating her in this endeavor?'' Though phrased as a question, Ryan knew very well it wasn't.

He shrugged. ''Probably, but I guess I'll work around it if I have to.'' His continued employment might be contingent on doing that, and this job was everything to him right now.

Work was his life. It was all he had left, and damned if he planned to junk it over something like this. He'd just have to invent some busywork to keep the woman out of his way while he was doing what had to be done.

"Excellent." Lorenzo offered his hand and firmly shook Ryan's, then smiled in Nina Caruso's direction. "I shall tell the king that all systems are go. A space term for launching success, yes?" He raised an eyebrow at Ryan.

"Yes. Just before blastoff. Then everybody prays there's no malfunction," Ryan said wryly.

"I shall leave you both to it, then," Lorenzo said and exited as swiftly as he had entered.

The determined look on Nina Caruso's face instantly sobered Ryan's smile, as did the prospect of stumbling over a family member of the victim while he concentrated on finding a murderer. Lorenzo would stay out of his way and allow him to do what he'd been hired to do, but it was clear this woman wouldn't. Not when she had royal sanction to interfere.

"So, do I need to ask again for your consent in this?" she asked.

"Nope. Not necessary," Ryan said. "It's all in the way you put the question, I guess. A duke for backup definitely helped."

This was Ryan's first homicide in nearly a year. How was he supposed to give it his undivided attention and baby-sit at the same time? Nina Caruso was going to be trouble with a capital T, he just knew it.

In the first place, she was highly distracting. In the second place…she was highly distracting.

The phone rang. "Would you excuse me, please?" he asked her, looking meaningfully at the door.

Reluctantly she nodded and stepped just outside and closed it as Ryan answered, "McDonough."

"My, but you do sound put-upon, my friend." It was Lorenzo again, obviously calling from his cell phone.

"That's only because I am," Ryan said conversationally, then added the requisite, "Your Grace."

Lorenzo continued, speaking swiftly and much more seriously, "I had hoped to arrive before she did, but I was delayed. There was no time to arrange another audience with the king so that he could make you aware of the situation. He sent me to inform you that Nina Caruso is to be closely watched and that he wishes you to do this personally. Her motive for coming here bears careful scrutiny."

"Why is that? Her brother's dead and she came to find out what happened. Isn't that reason enough?"

Lorenzo issued a little hum of suspicion. "No one has yet determined who informed her of Desmond's death or why she arrived so soon after it occurred. She says an official from the palace phoned her, but this is not so. I volunteered to notify her myself, but she had already left to come here before I had the chance to call."

"She had prior knowledge, maybe conspired?" Ryan asked.

"Possibly. Find out and keep an eye on her while you do. A very close eye, my friend."

"Count on it."

INTIMATE MOMENTS™

presents:

Romancing the Crown

With the help of their powerful allies, the royal family of Montebello is determined to find their missing heir. But the search for the beloved prince is not without danger—or passion!

Available in September 2002:
A ROYAL MURDER
by Lyn Stone (IM #1172)

Murder brought beautiful Nina Caruso to Montebello in search of justice. But would her love for sexy P.I. Ryan McDonough help open her eyes to the shocking truth behind her brother's death?

This exciting series continues throughout the year with these fabulous titles:

Available only from Silhouette Intimate Moments
at your favorite retail outlet.

Where love comes alive™

Visit Silhouette at www.eHarlequin.com

SIMRC9

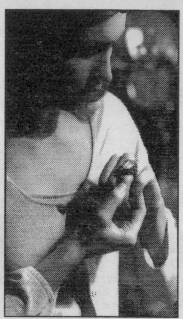

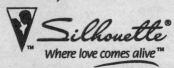

**Where royalty and romance
go hand in hand...**

The series continues in Silhouette Romance
with these unforgettable novels:

HER ROYAL HUSBAND
by Cara Colter
on sale July 2002 (SR #1600)

THE PRINCESS HAS AMNESIA!
by Patricia Thayer
on sale August 2002 (SR #1606)

SEARCHING FOR HER PRINCE
by Karen Rose Smith
on sale September 2002 (SR #1612)

And look for more Crown and Glory stories in
SILHOUETTE DESIRE starting in October 2002!

Available at your favorite retail outlet.

Where love comes alive™

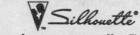

If you enjoyed what you just read,
then we've got an offer you can't resist!

Take 2 bestselling love stories FREE!

Plus get a FREE surprise gift!

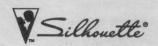

COMING NEXT MONTH